The soldier squeezed the trigger and the Desert Eagle roared

The second gunman swung his submachine gun in Bolan's direction, but the soldier already had his weapon fixed on him. He fired, scoring a direct hit in the gunman's face. His nose exploded in a splash of crimson, and his eyes rolled upward, as if trying to follow the path of the bullet that knifed through his skull to blow out the top of his head.

Bolan realized the table wouldn't stand up to heavy fire nor provide adequate cover when the enemy homed in on his position. He decided to change places and threw himself across the floor, skidding in behind another table.

A chair suddenly burst apart in front of him as a shotgun roared to life. The Executioner spotted the shotgunner. His adversary raised his weapon and jacked the pump action, a mistake made by a person obviously unfamiliar with combat shooting. Bolan capitalized on the error by rapidly trigg___ two rounds. The shotgunner spun like ___ ___ ___ he impact.

More attackers swa___

MACK BOLAN ®

The Executioner

DON PENDLETON'S
EXECUTIONER®
THE
ASIAN CRUCIBLE

A GOLD EAGLE BOOK FROM
WORLDWIDE.

TORONTO • NEW YORK • LONDON
AMSTERDAM • PARIS • SYDNEY • HAMBURG
STOCKHOLM • ATHENS • TOKYO • MILAN
MADRID • WARSAW • BUDAPEST • AUCKLAND

First edition May 1996
ISBN 0-373-64209-1

Special thanks and acknowledgment to
Bill Fieldhouse for his contribution to this work.

ASIAN CRUCIBLE

Alas, how strange it is that we are preparing to commit greatly sinful acts. Driven by the desire to enjoy royal happiness, we are intent on killing our kinsmen.

—The Bhagavad-Gita

War is always terrible. It may be necessary as a nation's collective self-defense or to enforce justice and stop the march of tyrants. Yet, we must never allow war to occur because ambitious and amoral individuals try to push us into battle to serve their own selfish goals.

—Mack Bolan

THE
MACK BOLAN®
LEGEND

Nothing less than a war could have fashioned the destiny of the man called Mack Bolan. Bolan earned the Executioner title in the jungle hell of Vietnam.

But this soldier also wore another name—Sergeant Mercy. He was so tagged because of the compassion he showed to wounded comrades-in-arms and Vietnamese civilians.

Mack Bolan's second tour of duty ended prematurely when he was given emergency leave to return home and bury his family, victims of the Mob. Then he declared a one-man war against the Mafia.

He confronted the Families head-on from coast to coast, and soon a hope of victory began to appear. But Bolan had broken society's every rule. That same society started gunning for this elusive warrior—to no avail.

So Bolan was offered amnesty to work within the system against terrorism. This time, as an employee of Uncle Sam, Bolan became Colonel John Phoenix. With a command center at Stony Man Farm in Virginia, he and his new allies—Able Team and Phoenix Force—waged relentless war on a new adversary: the KGB.

But when his one true love, April Rose, died at the hands of the Soviet terror machine, Bolan severed all ties with Establishment authority.

Now, after a lengthy lone-wolf struggle and much soul-searching, the Executioner has agreed to enter an "arm's-length" alliance with his government once more, reserving the right to pursue personal missions in his Everlasting War.

1

The Imperial Oasis boasted a regal title, but the place was a dump. Dirty sawdust littered the wooden floor, which was coming loose in several places and beginning to rot. Mack Bolan wondered how often they cleaned the place, but the smell of stale beer and moldy burritos didn't seem to bother the beefy, red-faced bartender. He leaned against a cushioned curve in the bar counter from where he could see the television set mounted above the shelves of bottles and keep an eye on the customers at the same time.

Bolan eyed the other patrons, half a dozen men dressed in black leather and motorcycle boots. They were assembled at one end of the bar. The youngest appeared to be in his mid-thirties while two seemed at least ten years older. Most of them boasted beer bellies, and they were in the process of downing their third pitcher of draft since Bolan's arrival.

The bikers grew loud as they talked about desert runs and beer busts. But one man, a goat-faced character with a polka-dot bandanna wrapped around his head, kept turning to peer at the Executioner. Bolan studiously avoided eye contact, watching instead the four other customers who were occupied at a table in a corner of the bar. Two of them had earlier hauled in large cardboard boxes, which they'd opened to reveal cartons of cigarettes. The larger of the pair now stood with his tattooed arms folded on his bared chest, while his smaller partner negotiated with the other two men at the table.

The four men glanced at Bolan with distrust. Although he was dressed casually—in a gray windbreaker, black T-shirt, loose-fitting pants and sneakers—he was obviously out of place. His clothes were clean, his rugged face clean-shaven and the fingernails of his strong, large hands well-kept. But Bolan hadn't come to the Imperial Oasis to arrest black marketeers.

He was there to meet Joshua Disher, and the man was late.

Bolan had never been fond of hanging out in bars, especially in a place that would have to improve to be considered a dive. Yet this remote watering hole in Imperial Valley—one of the least desirable desert regions in Southern California—was where Joshua Disher had agreed to meet.

When Bolan had first seen the files on Disher, he hadn't liked what he'd read, but this meeting was no social occasion. As if to remind the Executioner why he was there, a news report appeared on the television. The now-recognizable image of an emaciated figure filled the screen, as a news reporter delivered the commentary.

"Arlon Shaver spoke briefly at a press conference at the U.S. Embassy here in Bangkok, Thailand, earlier this morning. Two days ago Shaver was discovered along the border of Thailand and Laos. He'd been listed as missing in action in Vietnam since 1973, when he served as a sergeant in the United States Army. Shaver claims that he spent the past twenty-two years as a prisoner of war, shuffled from one jungle hellhole to another throughout Vietnam and Laos."

"Those goddamn gooks," one of the bikers growled. "We should have nuked the hell out of those bastards."

"We never should have been there in the first place," another man stated. "It was none of our business, and guys like this poor dude should never have had to go through this kind of crap."

"So you think we should've let them get away with this?"

"Hey!" the bartender yelled. "I'm tryin' to hear."

"Shaver's appearance occurs barely twenty-four hours after a reported border confrontation between Thai and Laos forces," the reporter's voice continued. "Thai officials claim their soldiers came under mortar attack by Laos forces. Laos still has close links with Vietnam and both countries remain under Communist rule."

The screen showed wounded Thai troopers being carried on stretchers from an ambulance to a hospital emergency entrance.

The reporter's solemn face replaced the visuals.

"This new aggression in Southeast Asia is causing international concern, but the governments of Laos and Vietnam deny Shaver's story, insisting they have no secret POW camps."

Bolan noticed the goat-faced biker's approach. He was swaying slightly, and he held on to the bar with one hand for balance. His voice was slurred as he spoke to the Executioner.

"And what do you think 'bout this?" he demanded. "You been real quiet over here, actin' too good to have anything to do with the rest of us."

"Hey, George!" another biker called out. "What are you doing?"

"I'm 'bout to kick this bastard's ass," George replied thickly.

The large biker came forward, moving quickly for such a heavy man. Bolan slid off the bar stool and slipped a hand inside his windbreaker. But the big guy reached for George, grabbing him by his jacket and pulling him away.

"Damn it, George!" he snapped. "Whenever we go on these bike trips you forget you're a shoe salesman and start behaving like you're Peter Fonda in one of those cheesy movies from the sixties!"

"Easy, Harry..." George began.

"If you get us into trouble with the cops because you can't control yourself after a few drinks..." the big biker warned. "Now, leave this guy alone. He's minding his own business, and you should do the same."

George frowned, then shambled back to the other bikers. Harry turned to Bolan and raised his hands in apology.

"I'm sorry, mister," he said. "George isn't a bad guy. He just gets a little carried away sometimes."

"It's okay," Bolan replied. "No harm done."

"Let me buy you another beer."

"Thanks, but I have to leave soon."

"Well, if you change your mind let me know," Harry said.

The telephone behind the bar rang, and the bartender picked it up.

"Imperial Oasis," he said. "Oh, yeah, Josh. What? No. Nobody's been asking about you."

"Disher!" Bolan said suddenly.

"Too late mister, he hung up," the bartender stated.

Obviously Disher wasn't going to show now, and there seemed to be no point in remaining in the bar.

Bolan was preparing to leave when the two black marketeers approached him. The bigger man with the tattooed forearms marched forward and thrust a finger at Bolan.

"Hey, wait a minute! What do you want with Josh?"

"You might let him know that if he wants help, he'd better contact us again," Bolan replied.

"Contact who?" the man asked as he stepped closer.

"He'll know."

"Perhaps you'd better tell us, or we could just beat it out of you."

He lunged for Bolan, his hands aiming for the throat. The Executioner met the attack, quickly snaring the man's wrist with one hand while his other swung a short chop to the side of the hoodlum's neck. The thug slumped to the floor.

The Executioner hadn't forgotten the second man, and he had no trouble dodging the wild roundhouse punch when it came. Bolan drove a hard right into his solar plexus. His left then scored a solid hook to the guy's jaw that sent him crashing into the bar counter.

The two men who'd come to buy cigarettes had risen from their chairs, but made no further move when they saw the compact Heckler & Koch P-7 pistol Bolan withdrew from inside his windbreaker.

"This isn't your problem," Bolan said. "Keep it that way and you'll live longer."

The pair slowly returned to their chairs. Bolan glanced at the bikers and the bartender. George looked as if he might be ill, apparently aware that he'd tried to pick a fight with a man who'd taken out two opponents in a matter of seconds.

The phone rang again.

"Answer it," Bolan suggested to the bartender. "Might be important."

He returned the H&K pistol to the holster under his windbreaker as the bartender picked up the phone.

"Josh! Don't hang up! There's a guy here..."

Bolan held out his hand, and the barman passed him the receiver.

"You were supposed to be here, Disher," Bolan said.

"Belasko? I heard someone call my name the first time I phoned. I called back as soon as I could."

"Where are you?"

"I'm right up the road," Disher replied. "About a mile north. You can't miss me."

"Good," Bolan said. "Stay put."

He passed the receiver to the bartender and headed for the exit.

Outside, the glare of the desert sun was fierce. Bolan fished the keys to the Jeep from his pocket, got in and started the engine. It was time to find Joshua Disher.

LESS THAN TWELVE HOURS had passed since Mack Bolan had first heard the name Joshua Disher. As the first reports of trouble in Southeast Asia came in, those at Stony Man Farm knew there was a good chance they'd have to get involved. And that meant the Executioner would almost certainly have another mission.

Bolan didn't relish the idea of another assignment to that part of the world. Too many ghosts of the past still lurked, and they always came closer to the surface the nearer he got to Vietnam.

Still, Bolan had met with Hal Brognola in the Stony Man War Room. The man from Justice sat at the conference table, chewing on an unlighted cigar. The Farm's resident computer expert, Aaron Kurtzman, a.k.a. the Bear, was also present.

Bolan studied the world map bolted to the wall. Numerous lights affixed to it signaled global trouble spots, making it look like a misshapen Christmas tree. Some had thought the world's ills would've subsided with the fall of the Soviet Union and communism. Yet Stony Man Farm was still in business and as busy as when the cold war was in full swing. Nowadays, it seemed as if every extremist group or would-be dictator figured it was time to make a power play.

"What's up?" Bolan asked.

"There's something strange about that business in Thailand," Kurtzman said. "You know we monitor surveillance satellites around the world—National Security Agency SIGINT, Central Intelligence spies in the skies, Organization of Naval Intelligence..."

"So what did we learn from monitoring all those sources?"

"That's just it," Kurtzman replied. "Not a single surveillance camera picked up a damn thing. Uncle Sam still has an interest in what goes on in Southeast Asia. So of course we have a fair amount of high-tech hardware around that general area. Then there's all the spy satellites the Russians, British, Japanese and others have sent up. We tap into some of those, as well. It's a pretty odd coincidence that this attack on the Thai troops just happened to occur when none of these satellites were in a position to observe it."

"Nor had there been any intelligence reports of an increase in military activity by Laotian troops before the attack," Brognola added. "And no evidence that Laos or Vietnam had been planning any sort of aggression toward Thailand."

"It's suspicious," Bolan agreed, "but acts of violence do occur along borders from time to time."

"But now this Arlon Shaver is claiming he's spent more than two decades in Communist POW camps in Vietnam and Laos. And then he just happened to escape and reach Thailand. It seems like a second mighty big coincidence on top of the first one."

"This makes for interesting speculation," Bolan said, "but we need something concrete to go on."

"We've been tapping into the major computer systems of all the national intelligence and military networks since this began," Kurtzman said. "About half an hour ago, a telephone call made from a pay phone in San Diego to the FBI national headquarters caught our attention. A guy calling himself Joshua Disher said he had information about Shaver and that somebody was trying to kill him to shut him up. I traced the call while he was trying to convince the FBI agent he was for real, and as soon as Disher hung up, I called the pay phone number and was able to get him on the line. I told him I was with a special division of the witness-protection program, and I wanted to hear more of what he had to say.

"Disher said he'd served in Vietnam with Shaver," the Bear went on. "I called up some information on Disher while we were speaking. He was in Nam and damn sure did know Shaver. They got caught dealing black-market goods in Saigon in 1971. They got heavy fines, were knocked down a rank and served thirty days in the stockades."

"So they weren't choirboys," Bolan said. "But it wasn't exactly high treason."

"Wait, there's more." Kurtzman reached for a file folder on the table. He handed it to Bolan. "Disher was nailed by the CID in Saigon for possession of heroin and was suspected of being a dealer."

Bolan studied the military 201 personnel file. The photo of a pale nineteen-year-old in uniform was attached to the top of the file. A separate sheet displayed a trio of mug shots of a slightly older Disher, with criminal charges listed below.

"At his court-martial he denied the dealer charges, claiming the heroin was for his personal use," Kurtzman said. "He was kicked out of the military with a general discharge and put into a treatment program for substance abuse."

As Bolan leafed through the file, he discovered Disher's face on more mug shots, his features showing the wear of time and abuse. In his most recent photograph, he had a shaggy beard streaked with gray.

"As you'll notice," Kurtzman went on, "Disher has been in trouble with the law quite a bit since he became a civilian. He's drifted around the country a lot and has never held a job for more than a few months. For a while he was on welfare and he spent some time on SSI, claiming disability due to delayed stress syndrome from Vietnam. He's been involved in a lot of petty crime, but that doesn't necessarily mean he's lying about Shaver.

"Disher says he wants to meet somebody face-to-face," Kurtzman continued. "He wants to be sure of protection before he gives all the details. I told him we'd send Special Agent Michael Belasko, whom he's agreed to meet alone at a bar called the Imperial Oasis."

"Okay," Bolan said. "I'll go talk to him and find out if there's any truth to his claims."

"We can't afford to overlook any possible lead," Brognola said. "The situation in Southeast Asia is hot and getting hotter. There are already voices in Congress and the Senate calling for military action. They want us to send U.S. troops into Thailand as soon as possible. A couple of major hawks are even saying we ought to prepare for war against Vietnam and Laos."

"And what direction is the President leaning toward?" Bolan asked.

"Toward Stony Man to help him," the big Fed answered. "You can imagine how worried the President is. He's looking at the possibility of the Vietnam War starting all over again. And I don't have to tell you how serious that is, Striker."

"No, you don't."

2

The briefing he'd had with Brognola and Kurtzman played through Bolan's mind as he drove away from the Imperial Oasis toward his meeting with Disher. He kept one hand on the steering wheel as he slipped the other into a small black bag he'd removed from under the front seat. He felt the familiar metal framework, trigger guard and grips of the Beretta 93-R.

He turned his full attention back to the road. It was worn by years of harsh conditions and in desperate need of repair. Sand flanked both sides of the road, and cacti and prairie shrubs dotted the landscape, with sand dunes forming small hills across the terrain.

Bolan saw no sign of anyone along the lonely desert road. He drove another mile before he saw a car parked on the shoulder of the road. The vehicle appeared to be a late-model Pontiac. A man stood by the open door at the driver's side and waved as the Jeep approached.

He was dressed in an old patched Army field jacket and threadbare cotton pants, with a sweat-stained baseball cap shading his eyes. Bolan recognized the bearded face from the most recent photos of Joshua Disher he'd seen in the Stony Man file. He brought the Jeep to a stop near the Pontiac.

"My car sort of overheated..." the man began.

Bolan stepped from the Jeep. "Knock it off, Disher. I'm Belasko."

"Uh... Do you have any ID?" Disher dropped his hand to the side of his field jacket and pushed it aside. Bolan stopped.

"You called us, Disher," he said bluntly. "I've come a long way to meet with you because you claim to have something important to tell us. If you're not going to cooperate, I'll just be on the next plane out of here."

"I just got to be careful," Disher muttered. "Somebody already tried to kill me."

Bolan suddenly drew the H&K pistol from his windbreaker, its short barrel pointed toward the sky. "If I wanted to kill you," he said, "you'd be dead by now. I have identification in my pocket. Do you really need to see it?''

Disher shook his head.

"I think I might be more comfortable if you take out whatever you've got hidden under your jacket and toss it over here."

The man hesitated, then slowly reached back and produced a dirty sweat sock with something stuffed in the toe. Its shape suggested it was a rock, perhaps slightly smaller than a tennis ball.

"An improvised blackjack?" Bolan asked. "That's it?"

"Yeah." Disher seemed embarrassed. "It's the only weapon I've been able to afford, but I've used this in street fights and it works better than you might think."

"Nice car," the Executioner remarked as he leathered the pistol. "Especially for a guy who can only afford an old sock with a rock in it to protect himself. When did you steal it?"

"Hey, I was desperate. I told you they tried to kill me once already. It happened the day after they announced Shaver showed up in Thailand. There's got to be a connection."

"I've read your rap sheet, so I'm sure you've made an enemy or two along the way. What makes you so sure an attempt on your life isn't just somebody trying to get even with you for a rip-off, or getting worked over with that poor man's blackjack?''

Disher shook his head violently. ''No way, man! The guys who came after me were pros. I was headed back to my room at this boarding-house in San Diego. I'm sort of behind on my rent, so I didn't want to get into any hassle with the landlord. I catfooted down the hall and saw two guys picking the lock to my door. Then one of them spotted me and pulled a piece. It was an expensive-looking automatic with a silencer attached. I jumped back and the bullet hit the wall just where my head had been. They didn't say anything, like 'there he is.' They just came after me. I hit the fire exit and made it into the alley. I squeezed behind a garbage Dumpster and hid in between some boxes. One of them popped the hood to the Dumpster and checked inside. Then I heard one of them say 'Pigeon flew. Check the street on your side. We'll get the other end.' Then a voice, over some static, came back, but I couldn't make out what was said.''

''A two-way radio unit and silencers,'' Bolan remarked. ''Doesn't sound like amateur night . . . if you're telling the truth.''

"Damn! What do I have to say to convince you?"

"We'll talk in the Jeep," Bolan replied. "We'll leave the stolen car here. We don't need the highway patrol asking about it."

"They don't cruise this area much," Disher said.

"You'd better hope not. And you'd better hope the guys after your scalp don't know you do business at the Imperial Oasis and decide to check the area."

"That's why I decided to stay outside and call instead," Disher said smugly.

"I don't see a pay phone around here, so you must've used a car phone in the hot Pontiac. Right?"

"Yeah. So what?"

"So mobile phones are basically a type of two-way radio with a pretty simple frequency level. They can be picked up on CB radio units, police scanners and even similar car phones. In other words somebody could have easily eavesdropped on your phone call, and they'd have a pretty good idea where to find you."

"Oh, hell..." Disher whispered, his eyes wide with fear.

"I suggest we get moving," Bolan told him.

Disher reached into the Pontiac and grabbed a paper bag loaded with whatever he'd brought for the trip. He climbed into the Jeep's passenger seat as Bolan stuffed his bag with the 93-R under the driver's seat. He started the engine, guided the vehicle off the shoulder and proceeded along the road.

"Tell me about Vietnam," Bolan said, his eyes scanning their surroundings.

"It was a living hell over there," Disher began. "You wouldn't believe what we went through in those goddamn jungles—"

"Spare me the war stories," Bolan interrupted. "I did my tour. From what I read in your 201 you spent most of your tour in Saigon and a lot of that in the stockade."

"Okay, okay. Shaver and I went to the stockade for black marketeering. I guess you know that. It was small-time stuff, and they didn't go too hard on us. Then we moved into something heavier."

"Drugs," Bolan said. He wasn't asking a question.

"Yeah," Disher admitted. "So you know I got bounced out of the service. But what you probably don't know is that Shaver was in on it.

Hell, he was my main supplier after his patrol was hit somewhere near Huong Te.''

"That's when Shaver disappeared and was first listed as MIA. You're telling me he was actually dealing drugs after that?''

"Damn right. He took advantage of that firefight to take off and go into hiding. Shaver figured he could get a good deal with a major Chinese gangster family that had branches in Laos, Burma and Thailand.''

"The Triad,'' Bolan commented.

"Yeah, that's what they call themselves. You know about them, huh?''

"I've heard them mentioned once or twice,'' Bolan answered. "So Shaver was a go-between for some heavy crime lords in the Golden Triangle. You figure that's what he's been up to all this time?''

"I know that's what he was doing when I was in the drug trade over there,'' Disher said.

"I'm surprised Shaver was so involved with the Triad. They tend to be pretty clannish and don't trust anyone outside their own group much.''

"Apparently they believed Shaver had some kind of connection with an undercover CIA operation that was involved in drug smuggling to raise funds for the anti-Communist forces in Southeast Asia.''

"CIA? Did Shaver tell you this?''

"Yeah. I got nailed by CID a couple months later and I didn't hear about him after that. I figured he'd probably gotten himself killed. I'd nearly forgotten about him until he popped up on the news with that POW story. Next thing I know I've got a couple of professional hit men trying to kill me.''

"And you think someone in the government, maybe CIA, is involved?'' Bolan said, his eyes drawn to the vehicle that had appeared in his rearview mirror.

"They found me pretty quickly, and I'm not exactly listed in the Yellow Pages,'' Disher replied. "What do you think?''

"I think you have reason to be concerned.''

Bolan couldn't make out the type of vehicle behind him, but it was sleek and black, and gaining on them fast.

"Maybe we both do,'' he added.

Bolan stepped on the gas pedal. The black car kept on coming, a screen of flying sand obscuring the faces of its occupants. But Bolan could discern two men in the front seat. Worse, he noticed a second vehicle trailing the black car.

"They're after us, Belasko!"

"Don't panic," Bolan ordered.

"There's no top to this thing! They're going to make me easy and blow us away!"

The Executioner didn't need Disher to explain the possible danger they faced. Of course the cars behind them might simply be some harmless motorists, but he doubted that.

Bolan glanced about for any available cover or something that might offer them an advantage. There was nothing except sand, dunes, some sagebrush and prickly pear cactus—no cover and no potential witnesses. It was a bad spot to attempt a defense, and an ideal spot for a killing.

The black car was obviously designed for speed, and Bolan knew he couldn't hope to outrun it in the Jeep—at least, not if he stayed on the road. He turned the steering wheel sharply and swung off the road to hit the sand at 70 mph. Disher shouted something, but Bolan didn't pay attention.

The explosive chatter of an automatic weapon erupted behind the Jeep, and bullets rang against the metal rim of the vehicle. Bolan glanced in his rearview mirror and saw the black car in pursuit across the desert. Flames spit from the muzzle of a short-barreled weapon held outside the passenger-side window.

Bolan then saw the second vehicle—a blue Ford Mustang—before sand swirled behind the Jeep in a low cloud, obscuring his vision.

The Executioner had no intention of being an easy target. The Jeep might not have been as fast, but it was designed for rugged terrain. He headed for the dunes, the vehicle plowing through a loose collection of sand. He saw the black car skid and whirl in a wild spin, but the blue rig continued the pursuit.

Bolan felt the Jeep rise as they reached another dune. It careened over the summit and landed hard, tires digging into the sand. Disher yelled a string of obscenities, which Bolan ignored and kept going. The Mustang stubbornly followed them, although smoke had begun to billow from under the hood.

The black car had recovered from its spin and had taken up the chase again. Bolan raced to the next dune. It was larger than the previous one, and the Jeep rose high on its rear tires. Bolan clenched his teeth and gripped the steering wheel hard. The vehicle seemed to hang in midair for a moment before it touched down, the impact jarring its two passengers. The Executioner managed to cling to the wheel and keep his foot on the pedal. The Jeep sped on as the Mustang rose to the peak of the mound. Its rear fender seemed to scrape the sand at the top of the dune before it toppled sideways. It then rolled onto its roof and slid down several yards, with all four tires whirling in the air.

When the black car tried to top the dune at a slower speed—the driver clearly afraid of tipping over as the Mustang had—it was left with less traction in the sand. The car rolled sluggishly over the top, but when it tried to descend the tires spun into the sand to dig a pit for the nose of the vehicle.

Bolan saw that both cars were temporarily disabled. He stopped the Jeep, jumped out of the vehicle and yanked the duffel bag from under the seat. He moved to the rear of the Jeep and knelt, his P-7 pistol held in a firm two-handed Weaver combat grip.

Disher dropped to the ground near Bolan.

A figure began to crawl from a window of the upside-down Mustang, an Uzi held in one hand. At the same time, a man emerged from the black car with an Ingram MAC-10 in his grasp and immediately opened fire. A stream of rounds bombarded the frame of the Jeep. The whine of ricochets sang above Bolan's head as he aimed the P-7 and squeezed off two shots.

Both 9 mm Parabellum rounds found their mark. The enemy gunman fell backward, arms splayed, the MAC-10 dropping from his grasp. The second man from the black car had taken cover behind the vehicle, and Bolan could see the guy with the Uzi at the side of his Mustang.

"You got an extra piece?" Disher asked.

"You said it's been a long time since you handled a gun," Bolan replied. "It's better if you just stay down."

"I don't have to be a good shot to distract them with a couple of rounds so you can get a better chance to pick them off."

Bolan hesitated for a second, then removed the Beretta 93-R from the bag and jacked the slide to chamber the first round. He handed Disher the smaller P-7.

"Make sure you stay behind cover," Bolan said. "Nothing fancy. Just fire a couple of rounds and then duck. Got it?"

"Don't worry, I'm not about to play hero."

Disher moved to the nose of the Jeep. He fired two shots in the general direction of the black car, but the Uzi gunner returned his fire, bullets sparking along the hood of the Jeep. Disher drew back, then whirled again and fired the P-7. The guy clasped his hand to his chest and slumped to the ground.

Disher seemed amazed by his marksmanship. Bolan yelled at him to duck, but Disher didn't respond fast enough. The remaining gunman by the black car opened fire with a MAC-10. The machine pistol spit out a rapid burst of 9 mm slugs and Disher spun, blood spurting from his chest and neck. Bolan immediately swung his Beretta toward the gunman and squeezed off a 3-round burst. The man's head snapped backward from the force of the Parabellum bullets.

Bolan stayed low as he moved toward Disher. The guy didn't move. His eyes seemed frozen open, and his tongue hung from his mouth. There was no point in attempting first aid. Josh Disher was dead.

Movement by the Mustang drew Bolan's attention. The fourth and last member of the hit team stumbled from the car. He held his left arm in a position of surrender, while his right arm hung brokenly by his side. He limped as he approached Bolan, and blood trickled from a gash across the bridge of his nose. He was well-muscled, roughly thirty-five years old, with close-clipped sandy hair and light-colored eyes.

Bolan trained his Beretta on the man. "Who are you working for?" he demanded.

"I'm hurt, man. I could have internal bleeding. Get me to a hospital, and I'll tell you anything you want to know."

"Answer me first."

"A guy who called himself Smith," the hit man grunted. "He hired us to waste Disher because of a drug deal he screwed up for the Mafia."

"Nice try," Bolan commented, "but that's garbage."

"I need a doctor..."

"Turn around," the Executioner said, "and start walking."

The gunman suddenly dropped to his knees, his body canted to the right. His "broken" arm moved, and his hand swung forward holding a Walther PPK.

Bolan squeezed the trigger of his Beretta. A trio of 9 mm rounds split a bloodied line up the gunman's face. He dropped to the ground, dead, before he could fire his pistol.

The Executioner lowered the 93-R. A corpse couldn't answer questions, and Bolan needed answers.

With the United States possibly facing a return engagement in Southeast Asia, the whole country would be needing some answers.

3

The young Marine sergeant checked the list of names on a clipboard at his watch desk. He found the name on the sheet, then leafed through the pages on the board to the photocopied ID card that matched the name and face.

"I thought I recognized you, Mr. Radke," the sergeant said. "As the chief of embassy security, of course you're on the list, but we do have to follow security procedures."

"I understand, Sergeant," Radke assured him. "After all, I'm the one who set up those procedures."

Radke stood about six feet tall, and his expensive tailored silk suit was designed to enhance his physique. He fixed his cool blue eyes on the sergeant. "This is a restricted area, and I want everybody on duty to take that very seriously."

"Yes, sir."

"I know your CO, and I plan to tell him you're doing a good job, Sergeant," Radke stated. "We've got a delicate situation here. We don't want the media and other damn civilians coming in here and screwing things up."

"No, sir."

Carson Radke smiled his approval. He made his way along the white-walled corridor. Only a small section of the embassy clinic had been restricted to isolate the special patient of the ward. Radke wanted to make sure the isolation continued until he was ready to end it.

He reached a door marked 22B and rapped on it, announcing himself. A thin, pained voice called out that the door was unlocked. Radke pulled open the door and stepped into the neat, sparsely furnished room.

Arlon Shaver lay on a hospital bed. He was sweating and his pajamas clung to his thin frame. Radke turned the latch on the door, securing it. "I told you to keep this locked," he said. "I don't want you opening it to any unauthorized personnel."

"Can't you see I'm sick?" Shaver replied. "I can't drag myself out of bed to open the goddamn door for anybody who comes here. The jarhead at the end of the hall is supposed to keep unauthorized people out.''

"And he's following orders, but we can't afford to make any mistakes. Only a few of us have keys to the door. So keep it locked from now on.''

"What do you want, Radke? I feel like hell, and I'd just as soon you left me alone right now.''

"Yes, you don't look good," Radke agreed. "Having trouble with your intestines again? I thought the dysentery was all cleared up.''

"I have malaria," Shaver ground out. "You ought to know that because you gave it to me, you bastard!''

Radke shrugged. "That was part of the deal. It would seem pretty odd if you'd spent the past twenty-two years in POW camps in the jungle and didn't have malaria.''

"Easy for you to say. The doc said I have a pretty bad case.''

"You were informed of what to expect when you got the injections of malaria and the other tropical diseases. If we're going to pull this off, we can't afford to make any mistakes.''

"This had better be worth it, Radke. You guys have put me through hell for the past six months. I nearly starved on that diet of rice, fish and boiled grass.''

''You had to pass the medical exams,'' Radke explained. ''We've been through this before. It was all necessary, and it's almost over now.''

''Not for me,'' Shaver complained. ''I'll have the effects of this for the rest of my life.''

''You'll get the best medical care,'' Radke re-assured him. ''And you'll return to America a hero. They'll probably have parades for you when you get back. You'll be on television shows, and they'll pay top dollar to interview you. Then there'll be the book rights to your story. You haven't been to America for a long time, Shaver. You won't believe who becomes celebrities these days.'' His tone became thoughtful. ''Actually the country's changed a lot since you were there. Crime is everywhere. Gangs run wild. The economy's in the gutter, and every week somebody goes insane and slaughters half a dozen people. That's the America you'll return to, to become a celebrity.''

''Maybe I'm better off staying here,'' Shaver said.

''It's too late for that. Besides, you've made enemies among some of the Triad. They'd have caught you sooner or later. This was your way out and you agreed to it. Don't worry about America. We're going to push it into making some changes."

"What you're planning is pretty crazy, Radke."

"The whole world is pretty crazy these days. That's exactly why this'll work. You just play your part and stick with the story we put together for you. Now, are you sure you haven't forgotten anything else we need to know about? You should have told us about Disher earlier."

"That was a long time ago. I figured Disher had probably drunk himself to death by now or gotten into heavy drugs."

"Well, he didn't," Radke said. "But we're taking care of him now."

"Just like that," Shaver said.

"Yes, just like that," Radke echoed. "There's too much at stake to let the life of a damn burn-out get in the way. Or anyone else's, for that matter."

"I get the picture," Shaver said. "You don't have to threaten me. I won't back out now, especially when it's finally going to pay off."

"Just remember that. Frankly I think you're a low-life deserter with no loyalty to anyone or anything except yourself. You deserve to be hanged for what you've done in the past, but now you're finally going to serve a useful purpose. You'll make up for your previous betrayal of America.''

"So, when do I get out of here?''

"It won't be much longer,'' Radke replied. "Just keep going over the story we put together. Repeat it over and over until you really believe it. That shouldn't be too hard. It's a more appealing story than the truth.''

"Guys like you specialize in twisting the truth,'' Shaver commented. "And yet you always find a way to justify it.''

"That's because the American government and its people can't accept the real truth.''

RADKE LEFT SHAVER'S quarters to discover the U.S. ambassador at the security station at the corridor. The Marine sergeant was at his post, a clipboard in hand. Paul Finley stood alongside the ambassador. Small-boned, Finley waited with arms folded across his narrow chest. His face was as expressionless as a professional poker player's. The ambassador, however, was clearly agitated.

"This Marine tells me my name isn't on the list of persons authorized to meet with Shaver,'' the ambassador said. "Your friend Finley is on that list, but I'm not?"

"Paul is deputy director of special security for operations here," Radke replied. "My second in command. Of course he's on the list."

"And you two think because you're CIA you run this embassy now?" the ambassador demanded.

"You're discussing classified information," Finley reminded the ambassador, his eyes resting momentarily on the sergeant.

"You mean the sergeant here?" the ambassador asked. "He and every Marine stationed at this embassy knows you two are CIA. They're not stupid. Just because you don't have it emblazoned on your ID cards doesn't mean everyone doesn't know what you are."

Radke moved closer to the ambassador. "I appreciate your position as the top diplomat for the United States government in Thailand," he began. "That's why you have access to reports concerning this matter from my department and from the medical and psychological teams attending Sergeant Shaver. However, this is also a matter that concerns the national security of the United States, which has potential beyond your diplomatic status and may involve other countries besides Thailand."

"You're overstepping your authority, Radke. This may be a crisis, but that doesn't give you or the CIA the right to declare martial law at this embassy."

"I suggest you make a complaint to the State Department. Complain to the White House, too, if you like. But do remember to tell the President that I'm going to considerable trouble to try to confirm Shaver's story before we allow the international press to interview him or we send him back to the United States. Once he's there, the President will have to come up with some sort of response to all the questions being asked about Shaver, and what he plans to do about Vietnam and Laos."

"I'm sure the President will be delighted you're so concerned with helping him make foreign policy decisions," the ambassador said sarcastically. "But I will make some formal complaints about your behavior. I've never liked the way you do your job, Radke. Ever since they sent you to this post you've been trying to increase your influence at the embassy, conducting activities that you claim had to remain confidential, while using your position as chief of security to protect yourself. You've only brought in people like Finley because they're your cronies."

"Paul Finley may be a long time associate of mine, but he's also highly qualified for the job. Both of us have far more experience and qualifications for our assignment here than you, Mr. Ambassador. That's why I don't think you'll get too far with any complaints about us. The President might be more inclined to listen to you whine, but I suspect he'll want professionals handling this matter, instead of someone appointed to his position because he specializes in political sycophancy."

The ambassador's face tightened with anger. He'd already made veiled accusations and threats. This was as far as he'd go with Radke.

"I believe this conversation is at an end," he said. "But we'll talk again, Mr. Radke."

"I look forward to it, Mr. Ambassador," the CIA officer replied. "By the way, Shaver isn't feeling well. I think it's malaria, but I'll have the doctor take a look at him. You'll have a full report on his condition by the end of the day."

"Make it within the next two hours," the ambassador countered.

"All right," Radke said with a nod. "It'll be on your desk by 1:00 p.m."

The ambassador turned on his heel and departed with as much dignity as possible. Radke smiled, allowing him this small victory. The ambassador wasn't stupid; he'd keep his word about contacting government departments and agencies to complain about Radke. He'd discover, though, that the complaints would gain him little sympathy. When America faced a genuine crisis, the government always valued intelligence sources over diplomatic egos.

Radke and Finley left the clinic and headed toward the main building of the embassy.

"How is Shaver holding up?" Finley asked.

"He's played his role well so far, and he'll keep doing so because it's in his best interests. He knows that if he becomes a liability it's easy enough to suffer a fatal side effect of one of those nasty jungle diseases he's had injected into his system. No, Shaver isn't a problem for now. Is there any word on Disher?"

"They found him," Finley said, "living in some boardinghouse and apparently claiming assistance due to dependency on drugs and alcohol."

"Our tax dollars in action," Radke said with a snort of disgust. "Has he been terminated?"

"He probably has by now. We haven't heard anything for sure, yet, but we don't want them sending too much information and arousing suspicions. But there's nothing to worry about. Disher's burned out so many brain cells by now that he probably doesn't even remember who Shaver is. And he's certainly not sharp enough to avoid four professionals. When they catch him, that'll be it. Disher will be like a lapdog against a pack of wolves."

"Until we know for sure he's dead, he's still a problem. I don't like loose ends. We need to move onto the next phase of this plan to make certain everyone believes there's a genuine threat from the Communists. If too much time passes since the border incident, they might figure it was an isolated thing, unless another occurs to insure the outrage of the American people. The government will have to take action then."

"If this works, we're going to be in the middle of a real storm, Carson."

"In the eye of a hurricane," Radke said thoughtfully.

4

Dot matrix images combined to create a face on the wall screen at the Stony Man Farm War Room. Mack Bolan recognized the face. He'd seen it in Imperial Valley and pumped three 9 mm Parabellum rounds through it.

"The guy's name is Jurgen," Aaron Kurtzman explained. His fingers moved rapidly over the keyboard of a laptop computer plugged into the mainframe. "Edgar Jurgen. I'll skip the early routine stuff. Jurgen becomes more interesting when he enlisted in the U.S. Marine Corps and saw action when U.S. forces invaded Grenada. It wasn't exactly a major military engagement, but it must've whet his appetite for more action because he left the Corps and then disappeared. According to the official records."

"And what did you find out that's not so readily available to the general public?" Bolan asked knowingly.

"Interpol discovered Jurgen in Singapore—involved with a gun-smuggling operation. He had a phony passport that claimed he was a Canadian citizen. Scotland Yard was informed, and they contacted our Justice Department. Then along came the CIA who told Justice to leave Jurgen alone because he was involved in a black bag operation the Company didn't care to explain in detail. Want to guess what the black bag operation was about? Here's a hint. It involved the Banking Commercial Corporation International."

"BCCI, of course," Bolan mused. "There was also corruption and dirty deals involved with that."

"You can say that again," Hal Brognola commented, leaning back in his chair. "At least seventy-two countries were connected with the BCCI one way or the other. The institution was responsible for huge money-laundering operations for criminal syndicates and various government agencies. And clients included Marcos in the Philippines, Noriega in Panama and Saddam Hussein in Iraq. Uncle Sam isn't clean either. Since BCCI was founded, at least three U.S. administrations have been associated with these deals to some degree. The best-known being the Iran-Contra scandal.''

"Let's not forget that intelligence networks around the world were participating in these money-laundering operations, which helped cover up covert financing for everything from arms deals and supporting revolutionaries, to narcotics trafficking and terrorist activities— including the CIA and the National Security Agency," Kurtzman added.

"And what dirty business was Jurgen part of in Singapore?" Bolan asked.

"That was an effort to supply arms to anti-Communist rebels within Vietnam. Seems to have been an off shoot of an original black bag operation to help support the *mujahadeen* forces fighting the Soviet occupation in Afghanistan at the time. Some of the *mujahadeen* raised funds to support their cause by selling opium. CIA and NSA helped them get these funds, even if they didn't directly participate in actually processing the opium into heroin and getting it on the market.''

"So the business in Singapore was more drug money to finance anti-Communist rebels," Bolan said.

"Well," Kurtzman began, "whatever was going on in Singapore connected with the anti-Communist movement and Jurgen didn't last long. CIA hadn't sanctioned it, so it seems a handful of Company boys had put the scheme together on their own. The operation was terminated, but it proves Jurgen had found work as a free-lance operative with the CIA. He finally returned to the United States about a year ago. He was supposedly unemployed, but he was obviously working for somebody when he came after you and Disher."

"I think that's a safe bet," Bolan said. "What about the other three who were with him?"

"Similar background to Jurgen's," the Bear answered. "Except there doesn't seem to be a direct link with them and any CIA black bag operations. They all spent some time in the military, and all worked with Jurgen as mercenaries and gunrunners."

"And finally as assassins," Brognola finished. "That was their last mistake. Unfortunately they managed to take out Disher before you ended their careers.''

''Unfortunately I didn't take any of them alive,'' Bolan said. ''Any idea who might have hired them?''

''Let me give you some background information first,'' Brognola began. ''The chief of embassy security in Thailand is a man named Carson Radke. He's pretty much taken charge of Shaver since the guy appeared along the Laos border. Also, as top CIA case officer, he spearheaded the investigation of the border attack by Laotians on Thai troops. He also used his influence with Thai military Intelligence to encourage patrols along the border after the incident. He even stressed the exact area where the Thai patrols actually found Shaver.''

''You ready for the real bombshell, Striker?'' Kurtzman cut in. ''Radke knew Jurgen. He was part of the operation selling drugs for guns and money in Singapore.''

''Radke sounds like somebody we should get to know better,'' Bolan observed.

Kurtzman's fingers danced across the keyboard. A new face appeared on the wall screen. Bolan gazed up at the features of Carson Radke.

"Radke seems to have had everything going for him since he was born," Kurtzman began. "His father was the executive vice president of an import-export company that handled a lot of business in the Far East. Young Carson spent part of his childhood in Hong Kong, Taiwan and Thailand, and went on to college and graduated with honors. His expertise was in Asian culture and language. He speaks and reads Thai, Vietnamese and both Mandarin and Cantonese Chinese."

"Pretty smart guy," Bolan remarked.

"Real smart," Brognola agreed. "CIA is always looking for talented guys like Radke. They recruited him right out of college, and he excelled in every category. Besides his language skills, Radke became an expert in surveillance, coding and decoding, computer telemetry and interrogation. About the only thing he didn't score high on was target shooting at the firing range. He's only an average shot with a pistol or rifle."

"Computer telemetry," Bolan said thoughtfully. "That would include gathering information from surveillance satellites. Radke's position in Thailand would mean he'd have access to the orbit patterns of all the CIA satellites that pass over Southeast Asia. Those spies in the sky would have supplied ample information about other satellites in the area—NSA, Russian, British, whatever—to know their orbit routines as well.''

"And that would explain why none of the satellites recorded the border attack by Laos on Thailand,'' Brognola said. "Radke could have timed the attack for when none of the satellites were in position to observe what really happened.''

"And since Radke's team handled the investigation of the attack site,'' Kurtzman said, picking up the thread, "he could've covered up evidence that would've exposed the truth about the incident. It's simple. Two groups of armed troops along a border, a couple of rounds fired with a grenade launcher or whatever at one side, and you got them shooting at each other, with both sides thinking the other started it.''

"Who does Radke's team consist of?'' Bolan asked.

Kurtzman punched some keys and brought up another face on the wall screen. "Paul Finley. He's a long-time associate of Radke's. They've worked together several times in the past, and Finley was sent to Thailand on

Radke's request. Chemistry major in college, he'd apparently planned to go into medical research before he was lured into the Company. Besides being skilled in forensic science and the chemical analysis of bomb sites, he's an expert in tropical diseases.''

"If he can handle the chemical analysis of bomb sites, he shouldn't have any trouble putting together explosives," Brognola said. "He could probably walk into the average kitchen, reach under the sink for household stuff and put together something with a lethal blast.''

Kurtzman worked the keyboard once more, and Finley was replaced with the face of another man. Appearing at least ten years younger than either Radke or Finley, the guy was clean-shaven, with clipped brown hair, hazel eyes and a surfer's tan. He displayed a boyish grin.

"Finally we have Robert Noble. Radke met him Stateside about a year ago and also requested him for the Thailand assignment. Sort of a strange choice. Besides the age difference— Radke is forty and Noble is twenty-six—the youngest member of this trio doesn't seem to have the intellect of Radke or Finley. He's smart of course. CIA doesn't recruit dummies. Still, he doesn't have any exceptional talents that make him stand out.''

"So why did Radke want him specifically?" Bolan asked.

"We're not sure," Kurtzman admitted. "Noble speaks fluent French, and apparently he's been learning Burmese. He's also a licensed pilot and mechanic. He used to work for his father's company. They manufactured wind-up toys and clocks. He's been with the Company for only a couple years. Still, it's an odd choice for Radke to pick for his team."

"If they're responsible for what's going on in Thailand, what's their motive? What can they hope to gain by something like this?" Bolan asked.

"That's hard to say from where we sit," Brognola replied, as he unwrapped a cigar. "But we did come across something of interest when Aaron ran a check on any unusual communications before and after the incident in Thailand."

Kurtzman opened a manila folder and quoted from a data printout sheet. "Last month, fifteen thousand British pounds sterling was wired from a bank in Bangkok to a Hong Kong account under the name of Peter Fine. Another deposit of ten thousand pounds was sent to the account of Roger Ninsson the same week, and yet another deposit of twenty thousand pounds was wired to the account of Carl Locke. I dug back a little further. Turns out hundreds of thousands of pounds have been transferred from Bangkok to the Hong Kong bank accounts under those three names.''

''And you think those accounts are actually Radke, Finley and Noble using cover names in Hong Kong?'' Bolan inquired.

''These accounts were opened after those three started their tour of duty at the U.S. Embassy in Bangkok. And I couldn't find any record of a Roger Ninsson currently living in Bangkok. Now, there is a British citizen named Karl Locke—spelled with a *K*, but he's a newsman with the BBC and has been there for only the past two months. There's also an American named Peter Fine who has been living in Thailand for almost twenty years. He works at a refugee camp for Cambodians and doesn't seem to care a hell of a lot about money.''

''If they're raking in that much cash, they must be involved in something pretty big and very profitable, and in Southeast Asia that means we're talking about either opium or gun-running. Probably opium," Bolan said.

"That's what we figure, too," Brognola agreed. "Radke has certainly spent enough time in the Far East to establish contacts with the Triad. That's probably how he found out about Shaver—if we can believe Disher's story that the guy slithered off during that firefight to become a dealer for one of the Chinese heroin syndicates in the golden Triangle."

"But we have no real proof that a high-ranking member of the CIA is involved in some kind of conspiracy, or that Shaver is a deserter and not really an escaped POW," Bolan stated.

"There's one other possible lead," Kurtzman said as he worked at the keyboard. "You recall I mentioned the four guys you blew away in the desert had formerly worked together as mercenaries or smugglers. They also worked with some other renegade types."

Yet another face appeared on the wall screen—angular-shaped with pockmarked cheeks and unkempt dark hair.

"This is Frank Tully," he explained. "He occasionally worked with Jurgen and possibly one or more of the others in Southeast Asia. According to Interpol, Tully had been involved in heroin trafficking for a while. They never actually caught him holding, but he was filmed hanging out with enough known Triad gangsters to be considered an undesirable and was deported from Thailand two years ago.''

"Thailand," Bolan mused. "That's interesting. Where is he now?''

"He's been working at a garage in Chicago for the past six months," Kurtzman replied.

"There's no evidence that he's been in contact with Jurgen or any of his old cronies from the smuggling days, but it's worth checking him out," Bolan said.

"You better use a different cover though," Brognola suggested. "The police in California are still investigating the shooting deaths at Imperial Valley, and the bartender at the Imperial Oasis remembered Disher calling and asking whether a Mike Belasko was looking for him. Better put the Belasko ID on the shelf until we settle this business.''

"I could go with ID from the Justice Department or maybe the Drug Enforcement Administration. Considering Tully's background, the DEA would have a reason to want to check on his present activities," Bolan said.

"Okay," Brognola replied. "Tully might be a dead end, but it's worth a try. I've got a feeling it won't take long for things to heat up. This situation is pushing a lot of people's buttons, and hot heads can unleash all kinds of hell."

5

The fighters clashed in the middle of the ring. One combatant swung a bare foot at the other man's ribs, but the kick didn't stop his opponent from delivering a hard jab with his gloved fist. The crowd cheered as one fighter grabbed the other's head with both hands and pumped a knee into the man's belly. He slammed his knee twice more into his opponent before snapping his head forward to butt him in the face.

Carson Radke didn't pay much attention to the match. He'd seen *muay thai,* or Thai kickboxing, many times before. The martial-art sport was extremely popular and never failed to draw large audiences, with locals and tourists filling the seats. But there were fewer non-Asians at this match than usual. Visitors already in Thailand were calling their trips short and heading for home, while others had canceled their plans, afraid that the country risked becoming a battleground.

Paul Finley watched the contest with his usual emotionless expression. One fighter had gained a clear advantage and was making the most of it, hammering away at his opponent with his fists. He ended the contest with a flying wheel-kick, leaping forward, then whirling in midair, with one leg extended. The side of his foot slammed into the man's face, sending him to the canvas, blood splurting from his mouth and nose.

The crowd bellowed its approval. The loser was carried from the ring as attendants cleaned the blood from the mat. Flutes and drums began the ceremonial preamble to the next match.

Radke consulted his wristwatch. "I'll meet you outside," he told Finley, who nodded in agreement. The chief of security slipped on a pair of gold-rimmed dark glasses and tugged at the brim of his straw hat.

He glanced at the crowd as he headed for the exit. One pair of eyes seemed to be fixed in his direction, and Radke glimpsed a woman with an oval-shaped face, dark almond-shaped eyes and a sensuous full mouth, features more Eurasian than Thai, before her long black hair swirled as she turned quickly away. With the vague, troubled feeling that he'd seen that pretty face somewhere before—perhaps a prostitute who frequented the area around the U.S. Embassy—Radke emerged from the stadium and walked to a nearby pottery shop. Although a sign in the window declared the place was closed, the door opened as he approached. An Asian with a thick black mustache that contrasted sharply with his shaved head, stood in the doorway.

"Hello, Mr. Leung," Radke greeted him. Leung was a Red Pole, a Triad enforcer, and Chou's right-hand man.

"Please enter, Mr. Radke," the man said in invitation.

As he waited for Leung to close and lock the door behind him, Radke glanced about the shop. Brightly decorated objects filled the glass shelves.

"Is Mr. Chou ready to receive me?" Radke asked.

"Of course," Leung replied. "He is always pleased to meet with you, and he welcomes your business, but he is less happy with the conduct of your friend, Mr. Noble."

The CIA officer frowned. "What did Noble do?"

"I believe Mr. Chou should discuss this. He will then decide if Mr. Noble leaves with you or with me."

Radke understood the implication. Despite his polite manner, Leung was an extremely dangerous man. As Chou's chief enforcer, killing people was a part of his job, and Leung did his job very well.

They passed through a beaded curtain into a back room, where Chou sat in an armchair as if he were on a throne, waiting to receive visitors. Middle-aged, portly with a double chin beneath a round face, Chou could have been mistaken for a successful banker. He wore one of his expensive British suits, which he had tailor-made on his numerous trips to London, complete with a houndstooth necktie.

Robert Noble was on his knees in a corner of the room. His hands were tied behind his back, and his shirtfront had been torn. Two young Chinese enforcers stood on either side of him. Noble's face registered relief when he saw Radke.

"Am I glad to see you—" he began.

His sentence was cut off abruptly as one of the enforcers kicked him in the stomach. Noble groaned in pain.

"Good afternoon, Mr. Radke," Chou said, his English accent clipped and precise. "Did you enjoy the fights?"

"Yes, thank you," Radke replied politely. "Mr. Noble has obviously done something to upset you. Should we deal with that, before we get on with our other business?"

"Mr. Noble paid a visit to one of my brothels, where he chose one of my best ladies for his entertainment. I regret to say he did not treat her well."

"It was no big deal," Noble muttered.

"Shut up, Bob," Radke ordered. "You've been told about this sort of behavior before. If you can't control yourself, you're going to wind up in the bay as shark food."

"I believe Mr. Leung is ready to do exactly that," Chou said. "He finds Mr. Noble's actions most ungentlemanly. I don't want him setting foot in any of my brothels again."

"You have my word on that," Radke assured him.

"Do you understand that, Bob?" Radke asked, turning to Noble. "You either restrain yourself, or I'll let Mr. Leung take care of you."

"Okay," Noble agreed darkly.

Chou barked some commands in Chinese. One of the enforcers produced a knife from under his shirt and cut the ropes that bound Noble's wrists. The young American slowly rose to his feet, but the circulation in his legs had obviously been affected by kneeling for hours and his limbs refused to support him. The enforcers grabbed his arms and hauled him to his feet.

Leung suddenly stepped forward and jabbed a short, fast punch to Noble's solar plexus. It didn't appear to be a hard blow, but Radke knew better. Leung was skilled in *wu shu* martial arts. Noble gasped and jackknifed from the punch. He would've collapsed onto the floor if the enforcers hadn't been holding him up.

"That's enough," Chou ordered. "Take him into the shop and keep him there until we've concluded our business."

Leung marched through the beaded curtain, followed by the two enforcers dragging Noble.

Chou turned to Radke. "That man is trouble. But we can take care of him for you."

"I had good reason for choosing Noble for this operation. If I didn't need him, I'd be glad to let Leung have his wish," Radke responded.

"Let us hope that he doesn't become a liability, Mr. Radke. But now, let us get down to business. Our arrangement has so far been mutually profitable. Your influence with the local authorities and connections with covert transportation sources have been helpful in getting my merchandise to foreign shores. You even introduced me to some new outlets and methods of making money I was previously unaware of, although I've been doing this for many years, as you know. Inherited the family business, so to speak. My father was in the trade, and his father before him, and so on. In fact, I can trace my ancestors' involvement in the opium trade to the seventeenth century. But I digress."

"You'll remember those lucrative days in the sixties when the CIA helped your Triad operations in Burma and here in Thailand," Radke said. "When I'm put in charge of all CIA operations in Southeast Asia, we'll be able to set up a network far bigger and better than any in the past. We'll also be able to crush the competition."

"You mean this rival heroin syndicate that's been giving me trouble for the past four months? Ethnic Chinese, like myself, have always run the Golden Triangle operations, but now this gang of local Thai dealers is trying to muscle into my territory."

"I can help you crush pests like that. You'll control all the other Triad outfits as well. In two years we'll literally own Southeast Asia."

"You make it sound easy," Chou said, "but it is a very dangerous enterprise. This gang war with the Thai riffraff places the lives of some of my best Red Poles in jeopardy. And if any of them are captured or killed and traced back to me, everyone from the Bangkok police, to Interpol and your country's DEA will be hunting me down. You're asking me to risk everything on this scheme you've brewed up."

"It's worked well so far," Radke said.

"So far all you've managed to do is take charge of investigations and keep that gutter rat Shaver from cracking."

"But I'm getting more cooperation from my government. They're giving me more authority and power. Even the ambassador can see his status diminishing in this crisis. He's complained to Washington, and he's been told to keep quiet and let me do my job. *I'm* in control, Mr. Chou, and I'm going to stay in control."

"Very well. I'll get you some men to carry out the next phase. However, I caution you about becoming overconfident. A wise man knows better than to assume others are fools."

Their business concluded for the moment, Radke emerged from the beaded curtain to find Robert Noble still being guarded by Leung and the other two Red Poles. Radke bowed curtly to Leung and turned to Noble. He swatted the younger Company man across the face. Noble yelped in surprise and pain.

"Damned idiot," Radke growled. "Let's get out of here before I change my mind and let Mr. Leung take your head off."

They stepped from the shop, and Radke glanced about for Finley. He spotted someone in a small yellow Toyota and recognized the Eurasian woman he'd seen in the stadium. She appeared to be holding a camera.

As her car quickly joined the traffic, Radke made a note of her license-plate number. Whoever she was, she seemed to be interested in Radke, and he had every intention of finding out why.

6

Chicago was only one of Bolan's many old battlegrounds, and memories of the past flooded in as he drove the Ford Taurus rental car along State Street. But he had different problems to deal with now.

The seek-and-destroy missions seemed to be getting more complicated, with terrorist organizations often part of conspiracies, sponsored by governments or government agencies.

Take, for example, this new situation, where it seemed possible that a high-ranking member of the CIA might be conspiring to push the United States into a military involvement in Southeast Asia. The CIA was supposed to be "the good guy," but it seemed that the list of who could be trusted was dwindling, while the ranks of potential enemies grew larger every day.

He tried to dismiss these thoughts as he searched for the Kangaroo Garage. The weather was sunny and clear and traffic moved smoothly. Suddenly he spotted a billboard-sized sign with a cartoon-style kangaroo sporting a wide grin and several mechanics' tools jutting from its pouch.

Bolan turned into the parking lot and brought the car to a stop near the main entrance. He climbed out and adjusted his jacket over the Beretta holstered under his left arm. He entered a small front office. A man sat behind a cheap plastic and aluminum desk, a coffee mug in one hand and a magazine in the other. He raised his balding head at Bolan's entry.

"What can we do for you, mister?"

"Do you have a guy named Frank Tully working here?" Bolan asked.

"That depends on who wants to know," the man replied.

Bolan fished an ID case from his pocket and flashed the badge.

"Federal officer with the Department of Justice. Either get Tully out here or take me to him."

"Uh, sure," the man began nervously.

He started to rise, at the same time sliding a hand under the desk. Bolan made a move toward his Beretta, but the man's hands came up empty. Instead, an alarm shrilled through the building.

"Fire!" the man shouted. "We've got to get out of here!"

He rushed toward Bolan, babbling about gasoline and explosive tanks used for welding. He reached out for the Executioner, but Bolan got to him first, pulling the man off-balance and slamming his back against the wall. The soldier drove a short, hard punch to the guy's chin, and he slid unconscious to the floor.

"Not even close to a convincing act," Bolan muttered as he drew the Beretta, screwing a customized sound suppressor onto the threaded muzzle of the pistol. He moved toward a door near the desk, the 93-R held ready. He pushed it open to find the mechanic workshop and bay area.

The alarm continued to blare as two men scrambled to remove the cover plate from an engine block, while a third hastily poured lighter fluid into a metal drum. None of them noticed Bolan's entrance, but the soldier recognized the guy by the metal drum from the photos at Stony

Man Farm. Frank Tully turned to get a book of matches, then saw the Executioner with his Beretta and froze in place.

"The fire drill's over," Bolan shouted over the alarm.

The two men by the engine block also realized they had company. One of them raised his hands in surrender, but the other hurled a wrench in Bolan's direction. He ducked, and the tool spun by in the air about a foot from his head.

Bolan dropped to a kneeling position and gripped his 93-R with both hands. As the wrench-thrower reached for a tool tray, the Executioner squeezed the trigger. The pistol barked a muffled report, and the man screamed. A single 9 mm slug hit him in the left hip, shattering bone and punching him to the concrete floor.

The mechanic with raised hands still did not move, although he glanced fearfully at the man who rolled about the floor, howling in pain. At the same time, Tully ripped at his coveralls, popping the snap buttons and reaching inside. Bolan quickly fired another Parabellum round into the drum beside Tully. The high-velocity bullet pierced the metal, and the resulting sparks caused the drenched rags in the container to ignite. As the flames rushed out of the drum, Tully raised his hands in defeat.

Bolan kept his pistol trained on Tully as he addressed the mechanic. "Get down on your stomach, with both hands in front of you so I can see them, and stay that way until we leave. Then I suggest you call an ambulance for your friend."

The guy complied with the commands. Then Bolan turned to Tully.

"Slow and easy," the Executioner instructed him. "Take your gun out and put it on the floor. No tricks. You try anything, and I'll take your arm off at the elbow."

Tully slowly removed a compact .380 automatic from his coveralls. He placed it on the floor, then raised his hands again. Bolan noticed a pan filled with thick motor oil, probably drained from a vehicle. He scooped up Tully's gun from the floor and deposited it in the oil pan.

"Just so you don't think about using it," Bolan said to the mechanic. "Even if it doesn't jam, the muzzle will still be clogged, and it'll probably blow up in your hand. Okay, Tully. Let's go."

"What do you want with me?" Tully asked, his eyes betraying his fear.

"I just need to talk to you," Bolan said. "I didn't expect it to be this much trouble. So let's go before I really get upset."

BOLAN HEADED WEST. Tully sat beside him, his hands cuffed behind his back and the safety belt strapped across his chest.

"So what were you and your buddies doing back there?" Bolan asked. "I know you used to be in the heroin trade. Are you smuggling drugs from state to state inside cars?"

"Who the hell are you?" Tully asked. "I never knew the DEA to have agents crazy enough to pull something like this."

"I'm asking the questions."

"I know my rights. You haven't arrested me," Tully said with a sneer. "I don't have to say anything. This is kidnapping, man."

"You know, I bet I could dump a body in the Des Plaines River, and it would float all the way down to Joliet before anybody found it."

Tully cursed under his breath. "There's no drugs," he said finally. "The garage is just a chop shop. We get stolen cars, change parts so they can't be traced by serial numbers and sell them to people who want cars they can use for... business."

"It's not hard to guess the sort of business that needs cars that can't be traced," Bolan said.

"So what are you into?" Tully asked. "And don't expect me to swallow that you're a cop. You wouldn't be doing this on your own if you were."

"My status with the federal government is a little hard to explain, so let's stick with you. I happen to know you're on parole, and you'll be in a lot of trouble if they find out about that chop shop. This'll be your third felony, and you could be put away for a long time on this one. Looks like you have a problem, Tully."

"And you want to make a deal?"

"You better take it. It's the best offer you'll get. I want information about when you were smuggling drugs for the Triad back in Southeast Asia. I want you to tell me about a guy named Edgar Jurgen, and anybody else you might recall from that time."

"Jurgen?" Tully asked. "He's a mercenary. Probably hired out as a hit man, as well. Is that who you're after?"

"We already got him," Bolan replied. "We'd have to hold a séance to talk to him now. So that's why I'm talking to you instead. Tell me about your deals with the Triad."

"I was pretty much a mule for a big shot named Chou. He has a lot of influence in the Golden Triangle, with operations in Burma and Laos, as well as in Thailand. Runs a number of other businesses, most of them legal, that he uses as fronts for heroin deals. He also runs guns, but heroin is his biggest money-maker."

"Did Jurgen know Chou?"

"No. Jurgen did some smuggling with me, but he never dealt directly with Chou."

"Did you ever happen to come across Arlon Shaver in Southeast Asia?"

"You mean that former POW who's been on TV? Was he running dope too?"

"We're looking into him," Bolan admitted. "That's the reason we're interested in you. So this could be a bigger and a better break than you deserve. You cooperate, Tully, and we'll help you get relocated. You'll have a chance for a brand-new life without a prison record hanging over your head and enough cash to live in reasonable comfort. Unless you decide to screw it up, of course."

"You mean a witness-protection program?" Tully said. "Doesn't sound so great to me."

"It'll beat spending the rest of your life in prison. You got three choices, Tully. Which one do you like?"

There was a long pause. Finally Tully spoke. "Do I at least get to decide which state I'm going to be relocated to?"

7

The President of the United States appeared on the communications computer wall screen in Stony Man Farm's War Room. He wore a white dress shirt without a necktie and seemed older and more drawn than the man the public usually saw on television.

"Hello, Hal," the President greeted Brognola. "I'm sure you can guess why I've called."

"I've a pretty good idea," the big Fed replied.

"Things are going crazy at the White House," the President went on. "I've got people advising me to send troops into Thailand immediately. Others are telling me to wait for Shaver to arrive, to talk to him personally before I make any decision, and some think I shouldn't send in military force even if Shaver's story is true. There's even talk of having bombers on standby to blast Vietnam and Laos at a moment's notice."

"All I can suggest is that you delay taking any action until we have more information," Brognola said.

"Hal, do you know what's happening in this country?" the President asked. "Rallies have been held by groups who demand we declare war, and groups that insist we keep out of Southeast Asia no matter what. Clashes between these prowar and propeace protestors have turned violent. So far nobody has been killed, but that's bound to change if things keep going on like this."

"Of course we appreciate the situation and what you have to deal with, Mr. President. We just don't have anything definite yet."

"When we spoke before, you said you were checking some possible leads. Have you made any progress with these?"

"We have a suspicion about who might be behind this, but we don't have enough evidence to prove anything yet. To charge in without any idea of what's going on would just make matters worse."

"You have access to intelligence sources of the CIA, NSA and other agencies. You can get them to supply you with agents, make connections with the Thai government...whatever you need," the President said.

"That may not help as much this time," Brognola remarked. "The individual we suspect is highly placed and well-connected within U.S. Intelligence."

"Someone in *our* network? So Laos and Vietnam may not be planning to expand into Thailand after all," the President mused.

"What I said was we *suspect* someone," Brognola cautioned.

"But you people specialize in direct action, not intelligence gathering."

"This time we'll have to pretty much handle everything on our own. We can't really trust anybody."

"When will you be able to tell me something more concrete?"

"I wish I could give you a timetable, but there's no saying how long something like this might take. However, we're concentrating most of our energies on this mission. And we've sent our best into the field."

"Striker?"

"Yes," Brognola confirmed. "I have to tell you though, Mr. President, I don't like the idea of sending him on a mission like this. He'll be entirely on his own this time. No contact with Stony Man Farm, no help within Thailand, and no weapons, communications or surveillance gear. He'll have to play it all by ear."

"And he agreed to do it?"

"Hell," the big Fed replied, "it was his idea."

MACK BOLAN INSPECTED the passport. The name under his photo read Patrick Baum, United States citizen, resident of the state of Illinois and a frequent visitor to a number of Central and South American countries. Aaron Kurtzman handed him a visa, a driver's license and a credit card, all made out in the name of Patrick Baum.

"We've inputted data to the computer files of the DEA and FBI covering Mr. Baum's alleged gunrunning and smuggling activities and his work as a mercenary," the Bear said.

"I've obviously been pretty bad," Bolan remarked dryly.

"You bet. In fact Baum is so bad, we're not going to pipe in any records to the Customs Department or Justice until after you reach Thailand, because they may not even let you leave the States with a shady background like the one we've planted for you as Baum."

"Let's hope I don't get deported as an undesirable before I get a chance to carry out the mission," Bolan said.

"That's the least of your worries," Brognola said around the cigar jammed in a corner of his mouth. "You're going to be messing with the Triad, as well as with whatever Radke's put together over there. The last thing we need is for them to suspect you're a plant."

"I know. Chou has been a Triad leader for a long time, and he hasn't managed that by being stupid or careless."

"All the information we've been able to gather on Chou supports what Tully told you about him," Kurtzman said. "Interpol investigated him a while back. So did the DEA. They know he's connected to the heroin trade, but they've never had enough proof to haul him in. His wealth and influence have also been excellent insurance.

"The most recent information we have from Thailand suggests there's a gang war going on between the ethnic Chinese Triad—who've always run the opium trade in the Golden Triangle—and Thai crime syndicates trying to take control of the market. Chou's profit appears to be involved in this, so it may be more difficult to contact him.''

''But maybe now he'll be more inclined to make contact with somebody outside Thailand, because he'll figure that person isn't likely to be connected to the Thai gangs,'' Bolan said. ''Chou also seemed to trust Tully to some degree and accepted him as a Triad mule. I think I can make as good an impression as he did.''

''Maybe Chou just likes his mules dumb,'' Brognola muttered.

''I get the feeling you're trying to discourage me, Hal,'' said Bolan.

''Damn right I am. Not that I think it'll work. But I don't like the idea of your going into this situation alone.''

''I know, but we can't sit back and trust the government to deal with this mess. The politicians will waste time arguing about what to do while trying to blame each other. The bureaucracies aren't any better—the CIA among them, and we're pretty sure one of their most influential case officers is involved. We can't pass on this one, Hal,'' Bolan responded.

Brognola sighed. ''It's your show, Striker. Just make sure it doesn't turn out to be your last.''

8

The boat's motor was cut, and its five male passengers used oars to paddle silently along the Mekong River, which separated Thailand from Laos and Cambodia. They wore conical hats made of woven rice reeds, undershirts and cotton trousers. Bags of grain covered the bottom of the boat.

Leung checked their progress by the moonlight. The Triad enforcer had volunteered for the mission, although Chou had tried to convince him not to, worried that he might lose his chief lieutenant.

With their disguise, they weren't out of place on the river, as no restrictions had been applied to the fishermen or traders who used the waterway. An inspection of Leung's boat, however, would have revealed the weapons and clothing hidden beneath the grain sacks. So far, their luck had held.

Leung spotted their target—a small military post. With the help of the moonlight, he could see the small pier where three military patrol boats were docked, the radio communications center, and a slightly larger wooden structure that housed the men stationed at the post.

He whispered orders to his men. They quickly slipped into green fatigue uniform shirts, replaced their conical hats with pith helmets, then gathered up their weapons. Leung picked up an AK-47. The assault rifle felt awkward in his hands. He disliked guns, preferring to use *wu shu,* where the combat was personal and honorable. Bullets struck from a distance, and he saw no honor in being able to flee, duck for cover, or shoot back if one happened to have a gun.

Two of the men loaded explosive warheads into Russian-made RPG rocket launchers, while the others armed themselves with Kalashnikov rifles. Leung made certain the magazine was in place before he chambered the first round and set the weapon on full-auto mode. His companions nodded their readiness.

The boat was approximately two hundred fifty meters from the pier when they launched their attack. An RPG rocket exploded onto the plankwalk with enough force to shatter the windows and tear loose the tar flaps from the roof of the nearby building.

Soldiers ran from the billets as soon as they heard the explosion. Leung and the Triad enforcers opened fire on the troops, and three men dropped immediately, their bodies torn by the slugs. The other soldiers rushed for cover as streams of automatic rounds continued to slash into the billets, shattering glass, dotting the face of the building with rows of jagged holes.

Leung cursed as he fired the last rounds from his magazine into the night sky. Unfamiliar with the recoil of an assault rifle, the barrel had climbed higher and faster than he'd expected, and he fumbled with the weapon as he tried to reload.

The second man armed with a rocket launcher fired another projectile at the site. The RPG missile was dead on target. The building spewed across the pier in a heap of smashed wood, accompanied by at least one bloodied corpse.

"Now, let's get the boats!" Leung yelled.

He chambered the first round of a fresh magazine as the Triad gunmen opened fire on the vessels, their bullets splintering the hulls of the patrol boats. Shots erupted from the other side as some of the soldiers returned fire. A slug punctured a sack next to Leung, and grain spilled onto the deck near his feet.

A Triad triggerman suddenly cried out and dropped to his knees, his hand clasped to his bullet-torn arm. Having achieved their objective, Leung shouted orders to retreat before they suffered any more injuries. The motor roared to life and they sped up the river, with Leung and two other Triad gunners continuing to fire at the site, discouraging pursuit by the soldiers.

The bombed-out post soon disappeared from view as the Triad members dumped the grain sacks overboard, lightening their load and allowing the boat to go faster.

"How badly is Feng wounded?" Leung asked, once they were a safe distance upriver.

A Triad member had wrapped a bandage from their first-aid kit around the injured man's upper arm.

"I think the bullet went straight through his arm," the man replied, "but he's lost a lot of blood."

"We'll get off the river soon, and then he'll get the medical attention he needs," Leung said.

"Do you think Mr. Chou will be pleased with our work?" another enforcer inquired.

"We did what we were told to do," Leung answered, "so Mr. Chou and those Americans should be happy. If not, the next time they can try to do better themselves."

JOAN WING ADJUSTED the lens of her Minolta camera and triggered the shutter, the flash throwing a light onto the smashed remains of the buildings. The dead and wounded had already been removed from the scene. Forensic investigators picked through the debris, while military policemen kept Wing and the other reporters at a distance.

Although the sky offered only the pale light of predawn, more than a dozen vehicles bathed the scene with the glare of their headlights. Television crews were present, equipped with bright spotlights, video cameras and boom microphones. The press had swarmed into Thailand when the Shaver story had broken, and they'd arrived at this post in force. American, British, French, German, Italian, Japanese and Swiss TV personnel jostled for the best positions. They bickered and complained until Wing felt as if she'd walked into a debate at the Tower of Babel.

She recognized the grim face of the CID inspector, as he avoided the reporters and headed toward a pair of Occidentals, standing with an army officer. Wing tracked the inspector's progress through the lens of her camera. She drew in a startled breath when she caught sight of one of the men.

Carson Radke had turned to speak with the inspector, and his face was in full view of Wing's camera. She instinctively snapped a picture. Radke blinked in the aftermath of the flash, then looked directly back at her. The CIA agent clearly didn't want to be photographed, and his features seemed to tighten when he saw her. Wing couldn't be sure whether he recognized her.

"Joanie!" a familiar voice sounded behind her. "Fancy meeting you here!"

She turned to see the grinning face of Ian Colby, a reporter for a London newspaper whose management couldn't seem to decide if it was a serious journalistic publication or a sleazy tabloid. Colby had a personality better suited for the latter.

"I didn't know you were in Thailand, Ian," she said.

"Oh, every reporter worth his ink is here," Colby declared. "So good to see you again, Joanie dear..."

He tried to plant his thick lips on her cheek, but she sidestepped and his kiss landed in her hair instead.

"It's good to see you too, Ian," Wing replied. "Is your wife here as well?"

"No, she's back in London. Say, are you still working for that Hong Kong weekly?"

"Yes. I've been with their Bangkok office for about a year now."

"You better see about getting back to Hong Kong, then," Colby said. "They're headed toward another war here at this rate. I don't know what's got into these people. Suddenly they want to start trouble with Thailand, and then they lose that Yank prisoner. It's quite a mess."

"Funny how things happen sometimes," Wing remarked distractedly, casting a glance at Radke.

"You got an eye for that bloke?" Colby asked. "He doesn't look like your type. He must have some pull, though, to be chatting up that Thai officer."

"He's with the American embassy," Wing said shortly. "By the way, how did you find out about this incident, Ian?"

"I was in a bar with some people from the BBC when they got a phone call. Somebody leaked it. Luckily for us, because the Thais and the Yanks would probably like to cover this up."

"Somebody definitely wants it made public," Wing said. "It looks like every journalist in Bangkok was notified and given directions on how to get here."

"Well, this is a big story and a disturbing one. Some Laotians or Vietnamese in a boat apparently attacked the station here for no reason."

"How do they know the attackers came from Laos or Vietnam?"

"Survivors described them. They were in uniform, even wearing those jungle pith helmets that the Vietnamese like."

"Doesn't it seem a little strange that the Laotians or Vietnamese would carry out an attack and not even try to disguise their identity?" Wing suggested.

"It's believed that they were disguised as farmers or fishermen or something like that first," Colby said.

"They were in disguise until just before they launched the attack, and *then* they changed into uniform so everyone would know who'd done it? That doesn't make much sense," she responded.

"Neither does picking a fight with Thailand when you know it's bound to bring the Yanks back here in force. But maybe they wanted everyone to know who was responsible."

"The governments of Laos and Vietnam denied any knowledge of the previous border attack."

"Would you expect them to admit to it?" Colby asked with a chuckle, apparently amused by her naive remark. "They also claimed they didn't have any POWs—something they're still trying to deny even since Shaver showed up."

"During the early eighties Vietnamese troops did try to cross the border into Thailand," Wing declared. "The government never denied those attempts."

"Really?" Colby said. "I wasn't aware of that. I'm surprised that wasn't a big story at the time."

"For some of us it was big," Wing said. "Especially for those opposed to communism or Western controls, because the Thai forces repelled the Vietnamese without the help of either the European or American military. I imagine that's why it wasn't a big story for you Westerners. Just as you've had far more media coverage and outrage about Bosnia and Sarajevo than the genocide carried out in Cambodia.''

Colby seemed uncomfortable with her remarks. ''Well, we're covering the story now.''

''Because one man emerged from the jungle and claimed he'd been a POW for the last twenty-odd years.''

''You don't believe he's telling the truth?''

''I just think the timing's a curious coincidence,'' she replied.

Wing didn't mention the more sinister ''coincidence'' she'd observed concerning Carson Radke. She knew the little pottery shop next to the stadium was owned by Chou. So when a CIA officer arranged a covert meeting at a Triad-run business, something shady had to be in progress. And when that same CIA officer was handling the Shaver case and kept showing up at every investigation of alleged attacks by the Communists, the series of coincidences became more disturbing, and potentially more dangerous.

Radke continued to speak with the inspector and the Thai colonel, but Wing caught him occasionally glancing at her. If he recognized her, that could only mean the danger might become a lot more personal than she'd anticipated.

The taxi ride from the airport into the city of Bangkok was a pleasant trip. Mack Bolan was no stranger to Thailand, and with English a common second language, he'd had no trouble finding a taxi driver who could understand him. After the necessary haggling, they agreed on a price.

Traffic was light, and Bolan assumed that the tourist trade had dropped—with fewer people wanting to take a vacation in a country that could suddenly become a war zone.

The capital city of Thailand soon appeared in all its paradoxical glory. Ornate pagodas, great green and gold temples and shrines stood beside modern apartment complexes and office buildings. A network of canals extend throughout Bangkok, which has earned the city the nickname "the Venice of Asia." Boats cruised the canals, and children cavorted happily in the water. Houses built on stilts lined the canals, and Bolan saw part of the floating market where merchants trade from boats and rafts.

Tricyclelike *samlors* shared the streets with motorized vehicles and bikers, while pedestrians covered the sidewalks, dressed in anything from the traditional *pa sin* full skirts worn by the women, to Western-style clothing. Buddhist monks, clad in their saffron robes, strolled among the crowds, and passersby frequently put money or food into the wooden bowls carried by many of them, required as they were to live solely on the generosity of others as part of their order's path to enlightenment.

The cab drove to the business district around Siam Square. Bolan spotted a sign in three languages that identified the Crystal Hotel. The driver brought the cab to a halt in front of the buildings.

Bolan leafed through the multicolored Thai currency and added three green twenty-baht notes to the price of the fare.

"Thank you very much, generous sir. My name is Kratai. I will be happy to be your driver any time during your stay in Bangkok."

"I'll be going out tonight," Bolan said, "sometime after seven o'clock. If you're here,

I'll be glad to have you for my driver. Do you know the city well?''

"I have lived here my entire life. I will be here tonight. This is certain.''

Bolan knew from past experience that crooked cabbies weren't uncommon in Bangkok and occasionally it could be downright dangerous to get into the wrong taxi. However, he needed a guide to help him get around the city. Hopefully Kratai would fill that need.

Bolan entered the hotel lobby. The desk clerk had his reservation under the name of Baum on record, and handed him a key and ordered a bellman to help him with his luggage.

A short elevator ride carried Bolan, the bellman and the luggage to the third floor. After the bellman had pointed out the bed, air conditioner, telephone, TV set and bathroom, and accepted a tip, he finally left.

Bolan locked the door, switched on the air conditioner and peeled off his gray windbreaker. The flight to Thailand had been a long one, and he was looking forward to a hot bath. He set his briefcase near the bed. He'd done his best to avoid arousing suspicion at customs. Due to drug smuggling, Thailand limited the amount of U.S. cash that could be brought into the country, but there were no restrictions on traveler's checks. Bolan had converted some of these into Thai baht, knowing that he could easily exchange more later on with the hotel cashier or any of the numerous money changer shops found throughout the city.

The soldier tried to relax, but he wasn't comfortable being basically unarmed in a potentially dangerous situation. For security reasons his only weapon was a Choate "Executive Letter Opener" in an ankle sheath. Made of hard plastic in the shape of a small double-edged dagger, the "letter opener" wasn't as sharp as a steel blade, but its point was reinforced by the thick spine in the center. But still, it wasn't much of a weapon, especially against an opponent armed with a firearm of any kind.

Bolan enjoyed a hot bath and headed for the bed. He set a small travel alarm clock on the nightstand, reluctant to contact the desk and let the clerk know he was going to sleep.

He lay down, closed his eyes and slipped into restful sleep.

HIS INTERNAL CLOCK woke him before the alarm at 6:15. Bolan stretched to work the stiffness from his muscles, then dressed in loose-fitting gray pants, a black cotton T-shirt and black tennis shoes. He strapped the letter opener and sheath onto his ankle before pulling on his windbreaker.

As he exited the hotel, Bolan recognized the battered blue sedan with the word *Taxi* printed across its side in English and Thai script. Kratai stood beside the car, puffing on a cigarette. He smiled when he saw Bolan.

"You are right on time, sir. Seven o'clock. I came early to be certain I would be here for you."

Bolan got into the cab, and Kratai slid behind the steering wheel.

"There will be cockfights tonight just outside the city," he said. "I am very good at guessing which bird will win in such contests. We could make a lot of money with a few wise bets."

"Cocks fighting to the death isn't exactly my idea of fun," Bolan said. "I'd rather eat poultry than watch them kill each other. A friend of mine told me they serve very good food at a Chinese restaurant called the China Jewel. Do you know it?"

"Yes, it is by the harbor. But that's not a good part of the city. Most Americans like the Golden Dragon Restaurant."

"I think I'll follow my friend's recommendation and go to the China Jewel. Figure out how much you want to take me there, then I want you to come back in two hours' time to pick me up."

"For that I must ask nine hundred baht," Kratai said.

"How about seven hundred?"

"Eight hundred and fifty?"

"Make it eight," Bolan replied. "On second thought, let's go back to nine. I want to make sure you remember to come back for me. It's probably not a good idea to get stranded at the port."

Kratai started the engine and the cab pulled away from the curb, merging with the traffic.

The smell of the sea grew stronger as the cab approached the port. Lights dotted the area, with taverns displaying a variety of neon signs and cheap, colorful decorations.

Kratai drew up outside the China Jewel, the restaurant's name written in Thai, English and Chinese characters across the wooden likeness of a gong surrounded by a serpentine dragon. Bolan got out and Kratai took off.

The interior of the restaurant was subdued, with dim ceiling lights, and the windows covered by thick red curtains. A solemn-faced maître d' escorted Bolan to a table. There were only a few customers present, but the waiter didn't seem any happier to see the big American than the maître d' had been. Bolan perused the menu, then placed his order.

A small pot of strong, hot Chinese tea arrived at his table, followed shortly by his meal. While he ate, Bolan took stock of his surroundings. The restaurant staff, as well as the other customers, appeared to be ethnic Chinese—as far as Bolan could tell from their overheard conversations, which sounded more Chinese than Thai to his ear. No one looked directly at Bolan, but they were obviously curious about him, casting him sidelong glances.

"The food was good, sir?" the maître d' asked when he came over with the bill.

"Everything was fine," Bolan replied. "I was told about this place by a friend of mine back in America. He got to know the owner, Mr. Chou."

"Mr. Chou?" the man echoed.

"Yeah," Bolan confirmed. "Is he here? I'd like to talk to him. Let him know how our mutual friend is doing."

"Mr. Chou is not here, sir," the maître d' replied. "He is the owner, but he seldom comes here."

"I know Mr. Chou is a very busy man," Bolan said. "Still, I hope to see him before I leave Bangkok. I'm staying at the Crystal Hotel at Siam Square. I plan to be here for at least two weeks. Perhaps longer, depending on how long it takes me to do some business. Maybe I'll get in touch with Mr. Chou before I leave."

Bolan hoped that his interest in meeting with Chou would reach the Triad boss's ears and that Chou would respond. The Executioner couldn't afford to move too fast or seem too eager, as Chou would certainly get suspicious.

But Bolan realized that he didn't have much time to spare. He'd heard about the attack on the Thai post, and he knew he'd have to make contact with Chou as fast as possible without blowing his cover. And hope that he would lead him to Radke.

The soldier stepped out of the restaurant as Kratai's cab rolled to a stop.

"Do you want to go back to the hotel?" Kratai asked as Bolan climbed in. "I know some places where you could meet nice ladies."

"No, thanks," Bolan replied. I'm not interested in chasing women right now."

"I understand," Kratai said. "What sort of things do you like to do, sir?"

"That depends on how much I've got on my mind at the time."

Bolan noticed that they'd left the main street and were driving through a seemingly deserted, poorly lighted area. Brick walls and wooden fences loomed on either side of the road.

"Where the hell are we?" Bolan demanded.

Kratai stepped sharply on the brake, bringing the cab to a halt. As figures emerged from the shadows to surround their vehicle, Kratai turned to Bolan.

"I am sorry, sir."

"Yeah," Bolan said. "Me, too."

He balled his left hand and delivered a backfisted stroke to Kratai's face. The driver fell sideways into the door, stunned by the blow.

A man appeared at the passenger-side door. Bolan gripped the backrest for support and launched a sidekick, his foot shooting through the open window and slamming into the attacker's face.

The soldier rolled over the backrest and landed in the front seat next to the still-unconscious Kratai. Careful to keep his head low, Bolan glimpsed movement through the windshield as another aggressor circled the cab. Drawing the letter opener from its ankle sheath with one hand, the Executioner reached for the door handle with the other.

He jumped out, the letter opener held in his fist like an ice pick. A figure armed with a wooden club immediately confronted him. Instinctively, Bolan ducked, and the attacker's club smashed into the roof of the car instead.

Bolan swung his arm in a high, fast arc, driving the point of the letter opener through the skin and muscle of the man's neck. The blade sank deep enough to cut into the carotid artery, and blood spurted from the wound as the man staggered backward. Leaving the letter opener stuck in the guy's neck, Bolan turned to face the other hoodlum. Blood trickled from his mashed-in mouth. Bolan guessed this was the man he'd kicked in the face, but the snarl that issued from his cut lips revealed that he had some fight left. The sudden glint of metal in his hand also warned Bolan that he planned to do more than punch him in the mouth to get even.

The blade flashed as the knifeman lunged for Bolan's belly. The soldier jabbed his left palm into the man's forearm to parry the attack. He grabbed the guy's shirtsleeve with his right hand and pulled him forward, increasing the attacker's own thrusting momentum. The man's face connected hard with the steel edge of the taxi roof, and he crashed to the sidewalk, the knife clattering uselessly beside him.

Bolan picked up the knife and examined it. It was similar to a Bowie, the single-edge blade thick and sharp, with a brass-knuckle guard.

He slid into the seat next to the cabbie. Kratai's eyelids fluttered and he moaned as he began to regain consciousness. Bolan grabbed his hair, yanked his head back and held the knife to his exposed throat.

"You set me up," Bolan growled. "Unless you want me to cut your head off, you'd better tell me what this is about."

"I bring fares to them," Kratai choked out. "They rob the customer, then give me ten percent later. It's just business."

"Not to me. I take this sort of thing personally."

"I need money badly. I'm in trouble with some people over gambling debts. I bet too much on the cockfights."

"So it's okay if I get killed because you gamble?"

"They wouldn't have killed you. They've never killed anyone I brought here before."

"Well, they won't be doing anything to anyone for a while," Bolan said.

"I didn't want to do it. I always brought fares I picked up at bars before. They would be drunk and wouldn't remember details. You seemed to have a lot of money, and I thought this would get me out of trouble with the gangsters I owe money to."

"Do you know many gangsters, Kratai? Perhaps a big shot named Chou?"

"Chou? Everybody knows who Mr. Chou is," the cabbie replied.

"You better not be lying to try and save your skin," Bolan said. "Tell me something about Chou so I know you're telling the truth."

"He owns that restaurant . . . the China Jewel," Kratai stated. "He owns businesses all over the city. He deals in drugs, guns and other things. And he dresses like an English gentleman. He even speaks English with a British accent.''

"Okay," Bolan conceded, moving the knife away from Kratai's throat. "I think maybe we can make a deal."

Kratai sighed with relief and massaged his neck.

"First, I'm going to let you live," Bolan said. "Second, how much money do you owe?"

"Eight hundred baht."

"I'll give you five hundred baht now. And you'll get five hundred more when you help me make contact with Chou. Agreed?"

Kratai nodded his head vigorously. "I agree. I will help you."

10

The *Bangkok Gazette* had thrown open their offices to deal with the army of foreign journalists that had descended ever since Arlon Shaver had appeared on the scene. Joan Wing sat in a cubicle at a small desk with the telephone receiver pressed to her ear and a fax machine close by.

"You've sent us some good photographs," the voice of Chester Wong, an editor on her newspaper in Hong Kong, came over the phone. "But why have you included those taken in front of a kickboxing establishment, some sort of shop, a restaurant and apparently just a street corner."

"You'll notice all of those photos include either Carson Radke or Paul Finley, his second in command," Wing replied. "Some of the places they're at are owned by a Triad gangster named

Chou. I believe there's a connection between them."

"Hundreds of businesses in Bangkok are owned by the Triad," Wong said. "Hundreds here in Hong Kong, for that matter. You're not covering a crime story, Joan. Thailand could soon be at war with Laos and Vietnam. That's our main story, along with the American POW."

"But when anything happens, Radke seems to be there."

"We know he's CIA. Those Agency types often associate with shady characters. They get information that way. We journalists do the same thing from time to time."

"It's more than that," Wing insisted. "Doesn't it seem odd that Radke visits an obscure pottery shop that's owned by Chou and used as a cover for criminal actions, and the following night a Thai base is attacked by alleged Laotian or Vietnamese troops?"

"The Triad has a lot of power, but I doubt that even they can control the military actions of either Laos or Vietnam," Wong said. "All the evidence suggests the Thais were attacked by Communist troops. There were eyewitnesses who saw their uniforms and helmets. Forensic investigations confirm that the bullets fired were from AK-47 assault rifles, which are standard weapons in both Laos and Vietnam. Shell fragments prove that the rocket launcher used was a Russian-made RPG. I might remind you I'm reading this information from your own text, Joan."

"And let me remind you that those weapons and ammunition are available through black market sources everywhere in the world. We know that Chou deals in guns as well as heroin, prostitution, smuggling, protection rackets and so forth. He'd have had no problem getting such weapons, and he could've had some of his enforcers pretend to be Communist troops. It does seem strange that the attackers disguised themselves as peasants while on the river, but then chose to put on uniforms just before they hit the base. Why advertise who you are?" Wing finished up.

"But why would the Triad want a war? They don't have anything to gain from an armed conflict. Why would Radke want to stir up trouble? And why would a Triad boss agree to something like this to please an American CIA agent? Can we answer any of those questions?

If not, then these are just some farfetched allegations that we can't publish."

"I know I have to get proof," Wing admitted, "but don't dismiss the possibility that I could be correct."

"Looking for a conspiracy involving the CIA and the Triad isn't your job," Wong stated. "The last thing we need is to incite the American government."

"We can't ignore the truth just because it's something the West doesn't want to look at."

"I have to applaud your sense of right and wrong. That's a trait sorely lacking in our field these days. But don't get idealistic on me."

Realizing it would be pointless to argue any longer, Wing got back to matters at hand. "I know you can't use some of the photos and text at the moment," she said, "but I want you to hold on to your copies just in case something happens to me during my investigation."

"Do you think your life's in danger?" Wong asked, concern evident in his voice. "In that case, maybe you should get out now, or at least back off from covering those gangsters."

"We can't just dismiss Radke. He could be the key to this so-called aggression by Laos and Vietnam. He headed the investigation of the first attack, he was at the scene of the second and he's been keeping Shaver on a short leash ever since he turned up. How can we turn our back when it might be possible to stop a war by exposing a single man's actions?''

"But there are others. What about Finley and the other one you mentioned—what's his name—Noble. They're also CIA. Then there's Chou and the Triad. If they're as dangerous as you think they are, they could get to you at any time and any place in Thailand.''

"That's a comforting thought," Wing replied dryly. "I promise I'll be careful." They said hurried goodbyes and hung up, then Wing emerged from the cubicle.

She adjusted the strap to her camera and dug in her purse for her car keys. She gazed across the poorly lit parking lot outside the *Gazette* office. It was almost ten o'clock, and she glanced about for the security guard who usually covered the lot. She couldn't see him. The area appeared to be deserted, and the parked vehicles seemed to take on new, sinister shapes in the shadows.

Wing was tempted to wait for someone to exit the building before she ventured out into the lot, but she was tired, and it was unlikely that anyone would appear soon. She squared her shoulders and made her way along the rows of cars, eager to reach her Toyota.

A figure suddenly stepped out from between two parked cars. A young, tough-looking Thai smiled at her, at the same time raising his hand to reveal a long, double-edged blade. Wing gasped, her spine constricting with fear. She took a step backward as the man advanced.

A voice came from behind her, and she turned her head, hoping to see the security guard. Instead, she faced another Asian youth, who lazily twirled a steel chain.

The men moved closer, trapping Wing between them. She tried to scream, but the sound seemed caught in her throat. She wanted to run, but realized they would probably be upon her before she could get very far.

"Hey!" a voice called out suddenly. "Over here!"

Wing's eyes widened with alarm when she recognized the new arrival. Carson Radke marched forward between the parked cars. He was dressed in a tailored gray suit and held a black pistol in his hand.

"Leave her alone," he ordered the youths. "Get out of here!"

The hoodlums eyed Radke's pistol, then bolted from the parking lot, their rubber-soled shoes echoing softly on the concrete. Radke opened his jacket and slipped his pistol into its belt holster. Although relieved that the thugs had fled, Wing didn't feel much safer alone with the CIA operative.

"Are you all right?" Radke asked.

"Yes," she replied. "Thank you, Mr.... ?"

"My name isn't important. I'm just glad I was here to help. You really should be more careful though," Radke went on. "Bangkok can be a dangerous place for a woman. Parking lots, the streets, even your own apartment—nowhere's really safe these days. I believe I've seen you before in some places that can get pretty rough. You've been lucky so far, but good luck has a limit."

"I think I get what you're saying," Wing said.

"I hope so. Things are getting hotter in Thailand. People are worried that a war might break out. You probably know what they're saying in the newspapers."

"I've read some articles."

"I've a feeling you might even have written some," Radke commented. "A lot of reporters are here from all over the world. And while I appreciate the desire of a good journalist to do her job, even the biggest story in the world won't do you much good if you're not alive to write it. My advice is to take what you have so far and go back home with it."

"Thanks for the advice. I have to go now."

"Please think about what I've said. It really would be best for everyone. Have a good night," Radke concluded.

Wing hurried to her car. She had trouble getting the door open, her hand shaking as she tried to insert the key. At last she opened the door and slid behind the steering wheel. She breathed deeply, trying to quiet her racing heart before she started the engine. She glanced in the rearview mirror. There was no sign of Radke.

"He sure knows how to deliver a message," she murmured.

ROCK MUSIC BLASTED from speakers mounted on the walls of the nightclub. It sounded vaguely familiar to Mack Bolan, and he suspected the song was a variation of an American hit.

Dancers gyrated on the floor, while three young women, clad only in shiny G-strings and high-heeled shoes, danced on small platforms at the bar section. Kratai watched their movements with appreciation.

"You should try this," Kratai said to Bolan as he raised a shot glass. "Rice whiskey. It's very popular here in Bangkok."

"Thanks," Bolan replied, "but I'll stick with this Thai beer."

Kratai had claimed that the nightclub was another Triad front and that he could introduce Bolan to a subboss of Chou's who ran the place. The Executioner had already noticed several beefy characters who patrolled the club. Bouncers, or possibly even Red Pole enforcers.

"We've been here for about half an hour," he remarked. "When do we meet this guy you say you know?"

"I'm not certain, sir," Kratai answered. "I don't think it will be much longer."

"Let's just hope it'll be before my patience runs out," Bolan said.

Just then three men approached their table. Two were muscle, dressed in sports jackets, T-shirts, baggy black trousers and sneakers. The choice of footgear was typical for Triad thugs— sneakers being better suited to martial arts than shoes.

The third man was small and wiry. A scrawny mustache gave his lean face a ratlike appearance. A white jacket with a high Mandarin collar sat on his narrow frame. Rings decorated his fingers, and a gold Rolex watch was strapped to his wrist. He smiled, displaying small even teeth.

"Good evening, Kratai," he said. "And you are Mr. Baum, I believe?" Without waiting for an answer, the man spoke to his bodyguards in rapid Chinese. They departed, and their boss slid into a chair across the table from Bolan.

"My name is Po. I am the manager. I believe you were asking after Mr. Chou, the owner."

"Word travels fast," Bolan said.

"What is your business in Bangkok, Mr. Baum, if I may be so bold as to ask?"

"I'm interested in exporting some merchandise from Thailand to the United States."

"Really?" Po asked with a raised eyebrow. "And what sort of merchandise might that be?"

"Whatever will make the biggest profit," Bolan replied. "Another thing I'd like to get my hands on is something for personal protection. Some street trash jumped me tonight. I could have been killed if they had guns, instead of just clubs and knives.''

"The streets of Bangkok can be dangerous," Po confirmed. He turned to Kratai. "Did you know that Mr. Baum was attacked this evening?"

"I was there when it happened," the cabbie replied.

"How unfortunate that Mr. Baum's first evening in Bangkok should be marred by such an incident. What sort of items would appeal to you, sir?" he asked Bolan.

"I like a 9 mm Beretta 93-R pistol, or an Israeli-made .44 Magnum Desert Eagle," Bolan replied. "I'd feel more comfortable with either or both of those handguns. I'd also like about a hundred and fifty rounds of ammunition for whichever weapon I can get, and at least three spare magazines."

"An unusual choice in firearms," Po mused. "I don't know much about guns myself, but those certainly sound like very formidable weapons. I wish you luck in getting one of those handguns for your safety while in Bangkok."

"Well, if you happen to hear of anyone selling such firearms I'd appreciate it if you'd mention my interest," Bolan said, playing out the game.

"I would have to give some sort of down payment to assure the person you really wanted to make a purchase and had the money to do so," Po hedged.

"Do you think this person would accept traveler's checks?"

"Everyone in Bangkok accepts traveler's checks."

Bolan took seven hundred dollars in traveler's checks from a clip in a pocket and signed them. Po slipped them into his inside jacket pocket.

"I'll see what I can do," he said. "Where can I contact you, Mr. Baum?"

"I'm staying at the Crystal Hotel, but then you already knew that. Just like you knew my name, although neither Kratai nor I mentioned it. In fact I didn't even mention it at the China Jewel, only what hotel I was staying at. That means you've already done some checking on me, Mr. Po."

"As you say," Po remarked with a smile, "word travels fast. I hope you enjoy your visit, Mr. Baum."

He rose and headed for the bar, where his bodyguards had been waiting.

Bolan turned to Kratai. "Let's go. There won't be any more business tonight so I might as well go back to the hotel."

"Yes, sir. You are happy with my work? I did help you contact an associate of Mr. Chou's," Kratai began eagerly.

"Yeah, but now we have to see if it'll pan out."

11

Bolan slept until dawn, then rose and exercised, making this workout longer and more vigorous than the one before. He performed a series of sit-ups and push-ups, including some on his fingertips and the knuckles of his fists to strengthen and toughen his hands.

He then did a series of *kata* or karate form exercises, practicing the punches, kicks and other striking techniques of the martial arts. His style was a combination of various schools of combat, including techniques from kung fu to judo, to Western boxing and ordinary street fighting. And he knew how to do them well.

But he also knew that fists and feet were never as fast as a bullet, and even the best martial artist in the world was no match for a willing killer with a decent firearm.

By seven-thirty, Bolan was ready for breakfast. Over a rather strange combination of fried eggs, rice noodles, fruit and coffee in the hotel restaurant, he scanned an English edition of the morning newspaper.

The headline announced that both Laos and Vietnam denied playing any part in the attack on the Thai patrol post. There was also a statement from the prime minister of Thailand that there was to be an increase in the number of troops and heavy weapons positioned along the border, as well as an encouraging reminder of how Thailand had repelled the Communists on a previous occasion.

In an opposing viewpoint others in parliament called for aid from the United Nations and from the United States. It was felt that the President of the United States had failed to take a firm stand on the issue, and he was getting criticism from all directions. Lastly, Arlon Shaver had been declared fit to travel and would be leaving Thailand on a military flight back to the United States. Cries for retaliation against Vietnam and Laos for allegedly lying about POWs still being held in those countries since the war continued to be made.

The possibility of another war in Vietnam had caused daily protests throughout the United States and even in parts of Western Europe, especially in those countries likely to participate in a combined UN military force. And as violence continued to erupt between protestors and police, numerous injuries and at least three deaths had been reported.

The situation was getting worse. Some speculated that North Korea would support Vietnam if another war broke out, renewing concern that North Korea had nuclear weapons. Nor had the possibility that mainland China would get involved been discounted by the political theorists. Just how bad could it get? Bolan hoped they wouldn't find out.

He returned to his room, somewhat frustrated that there was nothing he could do but wait for Chou to respond to the feelers he had put out. Of course it was possible Po would keep the money Bolan had given him, and he'd have to continue trying to make contact by visiting other establishments owned by Chou.

Yet, Bolan sensed he was on the right track. If Po had suspected he was an undercover DEA agent, he would have clammed up and refused to acknowledge he knew anyone named Chou.

But no matter how Chou and his cronies presented themselves, Bolan was relying on the fact that they were still criminals and suffered the one weakness common to them all—they were greedy. As long as he seemed useful and could increase both their profit and power, the Triad would associate with him. But if they had the slightest doubt, they would turn on him like sharks in a feeding frenzy.

A knock at the door drew Bolan's attention. He reached for the letter opener he'd retrieved from his encounter with the street thugs and opened the door a crack. An Asian man stood in the hall, a small bag clutched in his hand. "Mr. Baum?" the man inquired.

"That's right," Bolan replied with a nod. "What can I do for you?"

"I believe you talked to a friend of mine last night about a piece of machinery. A Mr. Po."

"Yes, I did. Please come in." Bolan opened the door wider, at the same time pocketing the letter opener.

The man entered the room, and the Executioner closed the door behind him. The stranger set down the bag, then turned to Bolan.

"When you had supper at the China Jewel and asked about Mr. Chou, you said that you'd learned of him from a fellow American. May I ask the name of this individual, sir?"

"Tully. Frank Tully."

"Oh, yes. I remember him. I am Mr. Leung."

"I recall Mr. Tully mentioning your name," Bolan said.

The Asian smiled and bowed sightly. "I am flattered that Mr. Tully remembered me."

"You made quite an impression on him."

That much was true. Tully had told Bolan that Leung was Chou's top enforcer and lieutenant. He gave the appearance of being a quiet, polite and generally pleasant individual, but Leung was extremely dangerous when he had to be. Tully had warned Bolan of Leung's lethal *wu shu* skills. He recalled an occasion when he saw Leung kill a man with two blows to the chest with his bare hands.

The Executioner had no trouble believing Tully. Leung was obviously confident enough to come alone to see Bolan. The enforcer acted like a gentleman, but Bolan recognized a killer when he saw one.

"Did Frank Tully tell you much about Mr. Chou?" Leung asked.

"Some," Bolan replied noncommittally. "Frank knew I'd been to Southeast Asia, so he liked to share his experiences. It gave us something in common."

"You've been to Thailand before?"

"Briefly. I spent most of my time in Vietnam."

"During the war?"

Bolan nodded. "Things haven't been going too well for me in the States, so I figured I'd come here and see if I could get some of the action Tully had when he was in Bangkok."

"Things have changed," Leung said. "You must know of the recent events here involving Thailand's relations with Vietnam and Laos, possible U.S. involvement and the rather disturbing matter about Mr. Shaver, the POW who escaped from Laos."

"Oh, yeah. It was all over this morning's edition of the newspaper."

"You do realize we must be extremely careful, Mr. Baum. I can't say how much business Mr. Chou will wish to pass on to you. The possibility of war means tighter security along the borders and ports. If this becomes an actual conflict, we may have to shut down certain operations due to the risk of bombs and cannon shells."

"I don't think fields of opium poppies will be a primary target by either side," Bolan said. "I believe a lot of people in America are ready to go to war because of Shaver's claims. They figure this means Vietnam lied about having American prisoners from the war."

"I would think you would find the idea of prisoners most disturbing, being a veteran yourself, Mr. Baum."

"Of course," Bolan replied. "But Shaver wasn't a POW. His story is garbage. They'll probably figure that out after he gets back to America. He's running a scam. He's not smart enough to pull off something like this for long."

Leung's calm features expressed surprise. "You sound as if you know him."

"Indirectly, plus I know his type," Bolan replied. "Like I said, I was in Nam. I spent most of my time in the jungle, playing hide-and-seek with the NVA and the VC. I was in Special Forces, and we did a lot of work with 'sneaky-pete' types—CIA, Army Intelligence and once in a while with the Criminal Investigation Department.

"I was part of a detail looking into soldiers' involved with smuggling heroin. Shaver had been a black marketeer for some time, and he fell under suspicion. We were ninety-eight percent sure he was a mule for one of the Golden Triangle outfits when he 'disappeared' on patrol. He was listed as Missing in Action, but we figured that was probably to avoid getting nailed for dealing. We reckoned he'd get himself killed eventually, so we wrote him off. We were pulling out of Nam, and nobody wanted to try to hunt down one jerk who would only make the Army look bad if we caught him, anyway."

"It's amazing that you should know so much about him," Leung said.

"It's amazing Shaver didn't wind up dead. Frankly, Mr. Leung, I don't care about Shaver one way or the other. I'm here to do business with Mr. Chou."

"And Mr. Chou is interested in doing business with you," Leung replied, gesturing toward the small bag he'd brought with him.

Bolan opened it. Inside, he found a large blue-black pistol with a thick barrel and a pebbled butt grip. He immediately recognized the Desert Eagle, but noticed the weapon was slightly smaller than the .44 Magnum he was accustomed to. Three boxes of 158-grain, .357 Magnum shells in the bag explained why.

"Your request was unusual," Leung explained. "I'm afraid we could not get either the Beretta 93-R or the Desert Eagle .44 Magnum. The .357 model was the best we could do."

"I'm not complaining," Bolan assured him. "This ought to do for now. I'm impressed that you came up with it on such short notice."

"We do the best we can," Leung said. "You should be careful where you go at night, although you seem to be able to handle yourself quite well, even without a gun. We heard that you were attacked, and you came out of it without a scratch. Most impressive, Mr. Baum."

"You people seem to know everything that goes on in Bangkok," Bolan remarked.

"We do our best," Leung said again. He bowed. "It was a pleasure to meet you, Mr. Baum. We'll be in touch."

12

Mack Bolan scanned the row of vehicles parked outside the hotel until he noticed the black taxi he'd been told to look out for. A tall man, dressed in black pants, a white shirt, cap and sunglasses, stood by the vehicle.

"Are you looking for a restaurant, sir?" he asked Bolan. "May I suggest the China Jewel? It's very good."

The other cabbies began to make their pitch to try to get Bolan's business, but the man was already motioning him toward his vehicle. Bolan had received a phone call about an hour before. Leung had been on the other end, inviting him for lunch at the China Jewel. Bolan got in the taxi, and it pulled away from the hotel.

"Nice car," Bolan remarked. "It doesn't look much like a cab. You don't even have a meter set up."

"Don't worry about the fare, Mr. Baum," the driver replied. "This ride is on Mr. Leung."

Bolan leaned back against the seat. He could feel the big Desert Eagle that he carried under his gray windbreaker, the spare magazines in the cargo pockets. He was glad to be armed again. When he'd disassembled the Eagle and examined the parts, he'd found it to be in excellent working order. In fact there hadn't been any sign of wear on the metal, which suggested the gun was brand-new.

The .357 Magnum cartridges were pretty good factory loads as well—two 50-round boxes of flat-nose lead wadcutters and one box of semijacketed hollowpoints—all 158-grain ammo. They would work well in a heavy, well-made weapon like the Desert Eagle. Still, Bolan would've felt better if he'd had a chance to fire a couple of rounds first, to familiarize himself with the accuracy, recoil and barrel pull of the weapon.

He'd "dutch loaded" the magazines—wadcutters and hollowpoint cartridges alternately placed. The letter opener was in his ankle sheath. Under the circumstances, Bolan was as well-armed as possible. Still, he hoped he wouldn't have to shoot his way out of whatever rendezvous Leung had arranged.

The trip was short, and soon Bolan recognized the gong-and-dragon sign in front of the China Jewel restaurant. He also noticed that no cars were parked in front of the establishment. A Closed sign in the window explained the reason.

Bolan got out of the cab, climbed the steps to the restaurant and entered. Mr. Leung met him at the door and bowed a polite greeting. The two men just behind him didn't appear half as friendly. The soldier recognized Carson Radke and Robert Noble from the photos he'd seen at Stony Man Farm.

"Hello, Mr. Baum," Radke said. "You don't mind a little company for lunch, do you?"

Bolan met Radke's eyes. They were icy.

"That depends on the company," Bolan replied, acting the part. "What the hell is this about?"

Radke moved his jacket aside to reveal a black SIG-Sauer 9 mm pistol. He placed his hand on the weapon but didn't withdraw it.

"Before we begin," he said, "I want you to lose that heat you're packing."

Bolan glanced at Leung. The Asian shrugged in apology. Noble pushed the Executioner against the wall. He nearly responded with a fist but managed to control his reflex.

"Spread-eagle, buddy," Noble barked. "Face the wall, hands flat against it and feet apart."

Bolan assumed the position. Noble patted him down and found the Desert Eagle. He removed the big pistol and continued the search. He discovered the letter opener and removed that, too.

"That's everything," Noble said to Radke.

Noble suddenly whipped the back of his hand into Bolan's testicles. As the soldier hissed from the sharp stinging pain, Noble chuckled.

"Okay, Baum," Radke said. "Turn around slowly."

As Bolan started to do so, Noble reached out to grab his collar. The Executioner's left forearm rose swiftly to knock the Company man's hand aside. He kept going and drove his right fist into Noble's liver. The younger man dropped to the floor, gasping from the blow.

"Nice punch," Radke commented. "Now back off and let him get up."

"Just as long as he keeps his hands off me," Bolan said.

Noble got up slowly, one hand clasped to his aching right side. He glared at Bolan, then made a move toward the Desert Eagle he'd jammed into his belt. Leung materialized suddenly beside the agent. He grabbed Noble's wrist with one hand, and jabbed the other into the side of the man's neck, his fingertips pressed tightly to his thumb to form a "white crane", his hand transformed into the punishingly painful "beak."

"If you have not had enough pain," Leung said, "I will be glad to give you more."

Noble screwed his eyes shut and clenched his teeth as Leung exerted pressure on his nerve center. Radke shook his head, and Leung let Noble go. The younger man massaged his neck.

"You've really embarrassed yourself, Bob," Radke said, "which doesn't reflect well on me. I want you to wait outside."

"But, Carson," Noble began.

"I will not lose face because of you," Radke said, cutting him off, his voice hard. "I'll talk to you later. Right now, I don't want to even look at you."

Noble sheepishly obeyed. He placed Bolan's weapons on a table, then slunk out the door.

"Does somebody want to tell me what this is about?" Bolan asked again.

"Sure," Radke replied. "Let's have a seat."

He canted his head toward another table, away from the weapons. Bolan followed Radke, and they sat down facing each other. Radke set his SIG-Sauer on the table, his hand resting on the steel frame.

"I'm sorry about Bob. He gets carried away at times. You did a good job knocking the wind out of his sails, so I won't apologize too hard."

"He's young," Bolan replied, "but he may not live to get much older if he keeps acting like that."

"Maybe not," Radke agreed, then went on briskly. "You're a U.S. citizen here in Thailand, and you have no business carrying that Israeli piece. That's enough to get you deported or thrown in prison. I hear Thai prisons aren't much fun."

"Prisons aren't fun anywhere," Bolan said. "So far, all I know is that you people have threatened me and had me searched. But I don't know who you are, or what you really want."

"We're with security for the United States Embassy here in Bangkok," Radke explained.

"Do they know you like to hang out at a Chinese restaurant that's run by a Triad boss, especially when the place is closed, and the only other person present is a Red Pole lieutenant?"

"You might say this is private business," Radke said. "Now, you made some comments to Mr. Leung earlier today about Arlon Shaver. Would you mind telling me what you said?"

"I'm sure Mr. Leung gave you a pretty accurate version. Anyway, I just had my doubts about his being a POW based on my own experience in Vietnam. That's about it, and I really don't care what he's up to. I'll also be happy to forget I ever met you and Bob if that'll get you guys off my back."

"Actually we haven't really got on your back yet. If we did, we'd probably break it. We did some checking on you, Baum. It's a pretty interesting file they have on you. You were a soldier's soldier in Special Forces. An expert in everything—small arms, hand-to-hand combat, demolitions, surveillance, communications. You've got letters of commendation, lots of medals for bravery and two Purple Hearts. You got more decorations than a Christmas tree."

"The funny thing about military awards," Bolan remarked, "is that they don't pay the rent or buy groceries."

"I'm surprised you didn't go into the CIA or the DEA, or some other Intelligence outfit with a background like yours."

"I got a couple of offers, but I turned them down. Watergate and the Church Commission were going on after I got out of the service. And seeing how CIA operations were being splashed all over the front page didn't exactly inspire confidence in the Company."

"That's what happens when damn politicians stick their noses in," Radke said bitterly. "It's hard to say how many good men back off from the Company because they figure those people in Washington would screw them over if they felt it might make them look good with some investigative committee."

"To tell you the truth, I'm not so big on politics," Bolan said. "I think the way Washington ordered us to handle the war in Vietnam was screwed up and kept us from winning. It got a lot of good people killed for nothing. When I got back to the States, I was treated like a leper. They didn't care much for us Vietnam vets in the seventies. Serving your country can be pretty damn thankless, so I decided to concentrate on serving my own interests instead.''

"I can understand that," Radke said. "If I remember correctly from your file, you were a mercenary for a while in Central America. Didn't you also smuggle guns to anti-Communist resistance fighters in Cambodia and Vietnam?"

"That didn't pay off too well," Bolan answered with a shrug. "They were the underdogs and we knew it was a long shot."

"I don't recall anything in your file to suggest you ever dealt in heroin trafficking. That's the main trade for the Triad. Why do you want to get into it now?" Radke asked.

"Somebody is going to sell it to anyone who's willing to pay a lot of money to get it. As long as there is a demand for drugs, there will always be a supply. I don't particularly want to do it, but I need to make big money and I'm just not that picky about how I do it anymore," Bolan responded.

"You seem to have a lot of talent, and I'm sure Mr. Chou will have something for you to do. The only problem is that I find you rather suspicious, Baum."

"And why is that?"

"You seem a little *too* gifted."

"Knowing you Company spy boys and the Triad are watching me like a fox by a rabbit hole makes *me* feel a little uncomfortable," Bolan said. "I guess we'll both just have to live with how we feel."

"Not necessarily," Radke replied. "Let's take your friend Kratai, for example."

"The cabdriver? He wasn't exactly a friend," Bolan said with a sneer.

"No, he wasn't, was he? Especially when he set you up to be ambushed by that gang. Kratai admitted to that when we questioned him about you. We had to know if what you'd told us was the truth. He also took you to that nightclub to meet Mr. Po. He overstepped his bounds doing that. He had no right to take a stranger there, especially an American, to meet with one of Mr. Chou's lieutenants."

"How thoroughly did you question him?" Bolan asked.

"Unfortunately, Kratai didn't survive," Radke answered. "But don't feel too bad about that. It could have been you. Anyway, you don't need him. We'll make sure you have transport to anywhere you want to go in Bangkok."

"You guys are great," Bolan said sarcastically. "So, are we going to eat while we're here?"

"Of course," the CIA man announced. "In fact, I'm going to fix it myself."

Radke rose from the table and gestured for Bolan to follow him to the kitchen. He reached for a heap of ground beef set on a table. A stack of sliced cheese, some hamburger buns and various condiments were also ready for his use. Radke began to shape some beef into a pattie as he spoke.

"How do you like your cheeseburgers?"

"Medium," Bolan replied. "Cheeseburgers in a Chinese restaurant prepared by a CIA agent," he snorted. "This is a new experience."

"I worked as a short-order cook when I was a teenager," Radke said. "It's the only job I've ever had that wasn't with the government. I still like to work the grill once in a while. Besides you get tired of Thai and Chinese food all the time."

"You must have spent a lot of time in the Orient."

"But I'm still an American and a patriot," Radke insisted. "Not everybody knows what a real patriot is. You may be one, Baum, even if you don't realize it.''

"Well, let me know if I meet your qualifications for patriotism,'' Bolan said.

"When I make up my mind about you,'' Radke assured him, ''you'll know. One way or the other.''

13

The Executioner felt basically pleased with the way things had gone. He'd not only made contact with Chou's Triad, but with Radke himself. The fact that he was still alive and had his .357 Magnum Desert Eagle returned to him meant he'd gained some degree of trust with both the Chinese gangsters and the renegade CIA officer.

Carson Radke was a piece of work, Bolan ruminated. He was up to his neck in heroin trafficking, conspiring to have people killed, and probably trying to start a war that would cause incredible death and destruction—yet he believed he was a patriotic American.

How much of this Radke really believed and how much had been for his benefit was not Bolan's concern at the moment. What he had to do, though, was maintain Radke's trust and convince him and the Triad that Patrick Baum was more useful alive than dead. The death of Kratai demonstrated how ruthless these people could be and how little regard they held for human life.

Things were moving faster than Bolan dared hope for. Maybe too fast. Radke would be watching him closely to see what he did next. He would probably try to find out about everybody Bolan talked to or telephoned. The Executioner would just have to be careful and wait for the other side to contact him. He wondered what their next move would be.

He also wondered who was following his taxi in a small yellow Toyota. The driver was pretty good. Bolan knew that a less experienced eye than his might not have noticed the car at all or realized it was a tail, as it dodged behind other vehicles or took time to catch up to avoid being obvious.

Bolan thought about the possibilities. He knew about a gang war between the Triad and local Thai gangsters in Bangkok. Or the DEA, Thai CID, Interpol, the local police and other law-enforcement agencies might have staked out an establishment known to be operated by a crime kingpin like Chou.

The Executioner had no desire to get into a gunfight in the middle of Bangkok in broad daylight. Aside from the risk to his own life and to those of innocent bystanders, if the police searched him and found his weapon, Bolan would be on his own. He could wind up in jail. More likely, he'd be expelled from Thailand as an undesirable. Either way, his mission would be terminated.

Whatever happened, he would have to deal with it. But the Toyota didn't attempt to get any closer as Bolan's car rolled to a halt outside the Crystal Hotel. The Executioner stepped out of the vehicle and watched it drive away. He then walked along the sidewalk, scanning the street. He soon spotted the yellow Toyota parked a few yards from the hotel.

A leg slid from the open door. A very nice leg, too, Bolan noted with appreciation. It was followed by another great leg, and then a woman, with a lovely oval face, framed by dark hair, emerged from the car.

Certain that she hadn't seen him, Bolan quickly headed into the hotel and took a seat in the lobby. He found an English newspaper and pretended to read it. As he'd anticipated, the pretty young woman, a camera slung around her neck, strolled through the door.

She made her way toward the front desk, and Bolan folded his newspaper and rose from his chair.

As the Executioner approached the desk, he could hear the woman addressing the clerk.

"I saw you drive up behind a cab I was in today," Bolan said to her. "You should be more careful. We wouldn't want you to have an accident."

Joan Wing muttered something under her breath, barely looking at Bolan as she spoke.

"She doesn't understand you, sir," the clerk said, translating.

"Maybe not, but please let her know what I said. Okay?"

Bolan had turned toward the elevators, but the woman's shout of "Hey, you!" in clear English stopped him.

"Would you like to explain why you were at the China Jewel restaurant today when the place was closed for business?" she asked. "And how you just happened to meet with two members of the U.S. Embassy security division, as well as the top aide to a Triad syndicate head named Chou?"

"I am an American citizen, so I guess I can meet with anybody from our embassy. But where I go for lunch isn't really any of your business, ma'am," Bolan replied with controlled politeness.

"It's everybody's business if you're part of a conspiracy," Wing retorted. "And you threatened me. That's the second one I've gotten lately, and I don't like it."

"I didn't threaten you. I just said you need to be careful."

"That's how the other threat was expressed, too."

"It wasn't made by me. We've never met before, have we? I knew I would have remembered you."

"Oh?" Wing's eyes flashed. "Is that supposed to be a compliment? Should I be flattered?"

"The odds are you're a reporter looking for a story. Maybe you should look someplace else, then," Bolan responded.

With those words, he stepped into the elevator. His last glimpse of the woman's face before the elevator doors closed took in eyes bright with anger and full lips pursed.

Bolan hoped the woman would keep away from the situation brewing in Bangkok. She was obviously smart and had put together at least part of the truth. Radke or the Triad had to have tried to scare her off before, but it was clear the lady was determined. That was dangerous. She'd probably get worse than a warning if she didn't back off.

So much for things going too well, Bolan thought ruefully. He should have known that something or someone would come along to complicate matters even more. But he also knew that he had to place the mission before any individual's life... including his own.

PAUL FINLEY SCROLLED through information on his computer screen. Carson Radke stood in the center of the office, arms extended as he went through the series of tai chi chuan exercises that he practiced daily.

"I've got that data on Patrick Baum's bank accounts," Finley called out to Radke. "He seems to have at least four accounts in four different banks in Illinois. He closed them all and transferred most of the money into traveler's checks. Some was wired to a bank in Singapore. This same bank also received funds wired from accounts in Ohio and Indiana. It's possible that Baum may have had other accounts in these states under false names. None of them held more than fifteen hundred dollars."

"He probably didn't want to put too much in any one bank account to avoid attracting suspicion," Radke said. "Most of Baum's income hasn't been exactly legal. Also, if the IRS questioned his income and decided to seize one or more bank account, he'd still have cash to fall back on."

"Well, he's accumulated more than a hundred thousand dollars over a period of almost twenty years. It's not bad, but it's still a long way from making him rich."

"So apparently he pulled everything he had into this venture in Thailand. He must have decided that by getting into the heroin or gunrunning trade out of Thailand for a while, he could earn four or five times what he's worked twenty years to make. He could do it, too. It might even earn him more than expected. Nice to retire with a million-dollar nest egg."

"Look how much it's already earned for you and me," Finley said. "We'll be retiring on a lot more than that. Well, there isn't anything here to suggest Baum might be working for NSA, DEA, Interpol or, needless to say, the Company. Apparently he really is a reasonably successful part-time mercenary and gunrunner. He must be smart, because he's never been caught."

Finley leaned back in his chair and stared up at the ceiling. "Baum knows Shaver is a fraud. We had that idiot Disher terminated for the same reason...and his was more suspicion than certainty. Baum is smarter, which makes him a greater threat to us."

"Or more valuable," Radke mused.

"Security is vital to this operation," Finley said. "The more people we bring into this business, the more can go wrong."

"I agree, and there's one unstable individual we'll have to terminate in the near future."

"I had my doubts about bringing Bob Noble from the beginning. Pity those psychological tests he had at Langley didn't pick up his sadistic streak."

"I told you what he did at the China Jewel. He was completely out of line, but Baum sure put him in his place."

"No wonder you like him," Finley remarked.

"Leung was ready to kill him. If we want to get rid of Bob, all we need to do is ask Chou to send Leung to take care of him. But we can't terminate him until he completes one more task for us. After that, I'll be glad to strike him off our team for good. And replace him with Baum.''

"Don't you think you're putting too much trust in this man too quickly?"

"You've seen Baum's record. He's an ace jungle combat warrior. He specialized in infiltrating enemy lines during the Vietnam War, and handled missions in North Vietnam and Laos. He also worked covert operations for Army Intelligence. That's experience none of us has, Paul."

"That was a long time ago."

"Believe me, this guy can still cut it. Besides, Baum would serve as an adviser more than a soldier in the field."

"I still think we should be very careful about trusting anyone at this point. Especially someone we barely know."

"I won't say I trust him yet," Radke replied, "but I do feel he may be very valuable to us. If we change our minds we can easily have him terminated."

"Mr. Baum may not be so easy to kill."

14

Carson Radke greeted Mack Bolan as he entered the China Jewel restaurant. The CIA chief of security wore a black silk suit, white shirt and houndstooth tie. When Bolan had received the phone call inviting him to a private dinner at the China Jewel, he'd been asked to wear a jacket and tie for the occasion. He'd purchased a loose-fitting dark blue suit, and the unaccustomed tie felt like a noose around his neck.

The China Jewel seemed different this night. A beefy man with a scar down one cheek had replaced the maître d' Bolan had met on his first visit. And if the telltale bulges under their white dinner jackets were anything to go by, the waiters were Red Poles.

Bolan was armed with the .357 Desert Eagle. He hadn't been frisked, which was a good sign, but he knew he couldn't afford to get overconfident. He'd stepped into a nest of scorpions, and the slightest mistake would bring out their stingers.

Although the restaurant was again closed to the public, there seemed to be a lot of people. Except for himself, Radke and Paul Finley—whom Bolan recognized from the file photos—everyone present clearly belonged to the Triad, including those posted at smaller tables that had been arranged at strategic points of the dining room.

A large table by a wall appeared to be reserved for the more important members of the Triad. Bolan recognized Leung, clad in a black mandarin jacket with gold trim, seated to the right of a middle-aged Asian—Chou, Bolan realized. The Triad boss gestured to them to join him.

"Okay, Baum," Radke said to Bolan, "this is the man you've come to meet."

Radke took a seat on Chou's left, followed by Finley, while Bolan sat next to Leung. There was silence until Radke made the introduction.

"Mr. Chou, this is Patrick Baum from the United States whom I told you about."

"Hopefully our meeting will prove to be a mutual pleasure," Chou said in his clipped accent. "So you're a friend of Mr. Tully's, and you're looking for some work here in Thailand?''

"Something like that," Bolan replied. "Frank Tully isn't exactly a friend of mine, but that's how I learned about you."

"How is Tully these days?" Chou asked.

"I haven't actually been in touch with him for about six months. I don't think he had much going on, but he was still getting by. Of course he couldn't come back to Thailand after they deported him, so I didn't mention I was planning to come here."

"Exactly who did you tell that you planned to come here?" Finley interrupted.

Bolan turned to address Finley. "You guys checked me out," he said. "You know I don't have a wife and family. There's no one really to tell anything to and no reason to tell anyone even if there was. Actually, there's nobody I'm going to miss that a nice big profit won't help make me forget."

"You can understand why we have to ask, because of what has happened here in Thailand recently," Chou said.

"I made my plans before this business with Vietnam or Laos started. In my passport I have a list of the shots I got for cholera and typhoid.

The date was a month before these incidents occurred. I also bought my plane ticket about the same time. You can check the dates if you like," Bolan added.

"We do know you transferred funds from banks in the U.S. to a bank in Singapore over a three-month period, according to your bank records," Finley said.

"You people really did check me out, didn't you?" Bolan remarked. "So, now you know about me, but I can't say the same about all of you."

"By the end of the evening, we'll either have come to an agreement of some sort or you'll be dead, Baum. It won't matter who we are then, will it?" Radke said, his tone matter-of-fact.

"If you decide to kill me, I'll do my best to take you and a couple others with me when I go. So whoever chisels your name on your headstone might want to know how to spell it right."

"Please," Chou interrupted, "talking about killing is poor dinner conversation. I hope everyone likes duck. It's a favorite of mine."

"I apologize, Mr. Chou," Radke said, "but I do find something else about Baum suspicious. The fact that he knows about Shaver."

"That again?" Bolan asked with frustration. "I'm sorry I ever mentioned it. Look, I never really met the guy when I was in Nam. There's even a vague chance that he was telling the truth, but when he disappeared on patrol, CID figured he'd faked it. They were pulling troops out and sending us back home, and we all pretty much forgot about Shaver after that."

"Do you remember the CID officer's name?"

"No, I don't. It was a Greek name. Everybody just called him Captain Olympics, because he was a bodybuilder."

"It doesn't really matter now, though, does it?" Chou said. "Shaver left today on a plane for the United States. He will soon be in Washington, D.C., where he will have to go through another series of tests and questions."

"But Baum is still here," Finley commented dryly.

"You guys must think I'm a mighty big threat to have so many bodyguards here," Bolan said. "All this just because I knew CID was suspicious of Shaver more than two decades ago?"

"The additional Red Pole security isn't because of you," Leung explained. "We have had problems with a Thai syndicate. Did you hear about that, Mr. Baum?"

"Word gets around."

"So far, everything you've told us checks out," Radke told Bolan. "For now, let's say we accept you into our circle. So tell us, what sort of work are you interested in doing?"

"To begin with, I'm not sure what U.S. Embassy security or the CIA has to do with all this, but as long as you're not getting in my way, I really don't care. My only objection to your involvement is your tying up my time and you have that half-wit Bob Noble working for you. Frankly I think he's a bigger liability than I would ever be."

"Don't worry about him," Radke replied. "After he's taken care of a final chore or two, Bob will no longer be a problem for anyone."

Chou addressed Bolan. "Actually most of my business does not involve these gentlemen from the American Embassy. They've taken an interest in you, Mr. Baum, but that doesn't mean you'll be working with them, or for them."

"As you probably know," Bolan began, "I've done some gunrunning in the past, and I've handled security for other smuggling operations. I've also worked as a bodyguard and done recon. To be honest, I've never been involved in drug trafficking. Still, I'm interested in making money, and I'm not terribly fastidious about what I have to do to make it."

"I'm sure we can find something for you," Chou pronounced. "Now I think we should eat."

He signaled at a waiter, who nodded and headed for the swing doors leading to the kitchen. He'd just crossed the threshold when the roar of automatic fire exploded from the kitchen. His bullet-riddled body hurtled back into the dining room, his white jacket stained bright with blood.

Bolan's response was immediate. He slid from his chair, dropped to one knee and withdrew the Desert Eagle. With the help of Leung and Radke, he lifted the table and tilted it sideways to act as a shield.

"Stay down and behind cover!" Bolan ordered.

The blast of a shotgun sounded from the front of the restaurant, and a Red Pole enforcer landed on the floor close to Bolan's position, his chest ripped open by the burst of buckshot.

Bolan felt the familiar rush of adrenaline. He peered across the sights of his Desert Eagle, the weapon held in a Weaver combat grip, its barrel braced along the edge of the tabletop.

Two figures darted into view. Wearing dark clothing, gloves and a variety of headgear, they were easily distinguishable from the formally clad Triad personnel. Bolan trained his pistol on an opponent wielding a British Sterling machine pistol. The soldier squeezed the trigger, and the Eagle roared. He saw his target fall backward, drilled dead center in the chest by the slug.

The second gunman swung his submachine gun in Bolan's direction, but the soldier already had his weapon fixed on him. He fired, scoring a direct hit in the gunman's face. His nose exploded in a splash of crimson, and his eyes rolled upward, as if trying to follow the path of the bullet that knifed through his skull to blow out the top of his head.

Bolan realized the table wouldn't stand up to heavy fire nor provide adequate cover when the enemy homed in on his position. He decided to change places, and threw himself across the floor, skidding in behind another table. He left toppled furniture in his wake, and a chair suddenly burst apart in front of him as a shotgun roared to life.

The Executioner spotted the shotgunner. His adversary raised his weapon and jacked the pump action, a mistake made by a person obviously unfamiliar with combat shooting. Knowing that the man should have moved the barrel to track his target instead, and working the pump from that angle, Bolan capitalized on the error by rapidly triggered two rounds. The shotgunner spun like a top from the impact of the double Magnum punch, then dropped to the floor in a lifeless heap.

More attackers swarmed into the dining hall. Chou's bodyguards exchanged fire with them, and bodies began to fall in response.

Armed only with handguns, Chou's forces were at a disadvantage. More than one had quickly burned up his five or six rounds. None carried speed loaders. The attacking force was clearly better armed, with full-auto weapons and shotguns. Despite Chou's concerns, his people hadn't been ready to meet this threat from their Thai rivals.

Bolan scrambled for cover at the base of a large glass-fronted cabinet that displayed a number of ceramic figures. Most of the glass had been shattered in the exchange of fire, and he swept the fragments aside. From where he crouched, he could see twin muzzle flames shooting out from behind the table where Chou, Leung and the two CIA agents still huddled for cover. Several bullet holes marred the tabletop, the slugs punching through the wooden shield.

The SIG-Sauers of the CIA agents slammed the life from an enemy triggerman with 9 mm rounds, but another Thai killer took aim at them with a Sterling Mk-4. The subgun was capable of chewing the table apart and slaughtering all four men. Protecting a pair of corrupt Company renegades and a couple of Triad gangsters was hardly typical for the Executioner, but for the moment he knew he needed them alive.

Bolan raised his Desert Eagle and squeezed off a single shot. The round tore into the side of the gunman's neck below his jawline, the exit wound spewing his blood across a nearby wall. The hood's reflexes triggered his Sterling. The recoil pulled the barrel high, and he sprayed half a dozen slugs into the ceiling before his body collapsed to the floor.

A burst of fire shattered a part of the cabinet and forced Bolan to duck for cover. He heard someone yell something in a foreign tongue that sounded like a command, and suddenly the remaining members of the Thai force charged what was left of the defenders. Their primary target had to be Chou, and he was still alive. They were running out of time if they intended to accomplish their goal before the police or other Triad forces arrived on the scene.

Bolan could see only two surviving Triad bodyguards, and one of them appeared to be wounded. Both had run out of bullets, and they held knives at the ready as their only weapons. From what he could tell, about eight Thai assassins remained.

The Executioner fired into the enemy charge, bringing down two more opponents. His last bullet struck the steel frame of a hardman's shotgun and sent the weapon hurtling from the startled man's grasp.

As Bolan ejected the spent magazine and reached for a fresh clip, a figure suddenly jumped in front of him. The man smiled as he pointed a snub-nosed revolver at Bolan's face. Instinctively the Executioner lashed out and chopped the heavy barrel of the Eagle across the man's wrist. Bone popped, and the revolver fell from his hand. An almost comical expression of surprise and pain replaced his previous arrogant look.

A fast roundhouse kick caught Bolan in the ribs, knocking him into the side of the cabinet. The Thai hardman was neither a coward nor a quitter, for despite his broken wrist, he reached for Bolan's throat with both hands. The warrior's forearms rose to block the attack. He followed it with a solid left hook to the man's jaw. The punch spun him, and Bolan slammed the base of his skull with the gun barrel.

The hardman fell facefirst to the floor, and Bolan turned to deal with a second attacker. The Thai swung a high kick, his foot striking Bolan's hand and knocking the Eagle from his grasp. His opponent then jabbed a fist at Bolan's face, but he managed to dodge the punch.

The man raised his fist again, pivoted and lashed out in a wheel-kick, aiming for Bolan's head. It was a fancy move, but one better suited to a sporting contest than to real combat. Bolan was able to weave away from the man's flashing foot, and he quickly moved in to thrust a hard left jab to his opponent's chin. The guy's head bounced from the punch, and the soldier hooked a right to his solar plexus.

Dazed and bloodied, the Thai still tried to swing a wild right cross at Bolan. The Executioner grabbed his adversary's arm and hurled him over his shoulder. The man crashed down, unconscious.

Only then did Bolan turn to take stock of what was happening behind him. A pistol-packing Thai had rushed to the edge of the up-ended table, his gun thrust at the figures behind it. Leung struck suddenly, as fast as a cobra. He grabbed the man's gun hand, forcing the pistol toward the ceiling, where it fired a harmless round into the plaster.

Then, still holding on to the man's hand, Leung twisted it viciously until the Thai screamed and the pistol dropped to the floor. The Red Pole rammed an elbow into the man's liver, and as he doubled up in pain, Leung swung a deadly chop to the back of his neck.

Radke had his hands full dealing with the last two Thai assassins. He fired his SIG-Sauer but only managed to wound them, hitting one in the stomach, the other in the arm.

The CIA man discarded his pistol and ground the heel of his hand into the man's breastbone, toppling him to the floor. He then delivered a vicious kick to the fallen man's injured arm.

The guy screamed with pain and tried to kick Radke. The Company man managed to grab his adversary's ankle and forced him onto his belly.

Radke then straddled the man's back, gripped the Thai's hair with one hand, while cupping his jaw with the other. Radke pulled sharply. Bolan heard bone crack and watched the Thai go limp.

The Executioner scooped up his pistol and reloaded, then scanned the area for movement. Bodies of the dead and wounded littered the dining room. Bolan didn't take a head count, but there were more than twenty figures on the floor. His eyes met Radke's, and the Company man nodded in approval.

Finley rose, his hands shaking as he tried to feed a fresh magazine into the butt of his SIG-Sauer. Leung shoved the table aside and helped Chou to his feet. The Chinese kingpin's face was pale, but he was uninjured. He held a small .32-caliber revolver in his pudgy fist as he made his way toward a wounded Thai who gripped his belly as he writhed on the floor. Chou aimed his revolver, then calmly shot the man in the back of the head. As he made to move on, Bolan addressed him.

"Shouldn't we get out of here?" he asked.

For a long moment, Chou glared at Bolan, his eyes narrowed. Then his expression lightened and he nodded.

"The authorities seldom come to this part of town, but there is no sense in taking chances," he said. "You proved to be a most able opponent, Mr. Baum," he continued. "I am in your debt."

Chou snapped some commands in Chinese to Leung and the other two enforcers, who nodded and bowed.

"Come on, Baum," Radke said to Bolan. "We'll give you a lift back to the hotel."

15

Paul Finley sat next to Carson Radke in the front seat of the car. The air conditioner was on high, but Finley still sweated.

"I've been in a couple of gunfights before," Radke said, breaking the silence, "but nothing quite that intense. You were certainly impressive, Baum. Hero of the hour. Chou was right about that."

"To be honest, my first thought was to keep myself alive," Bolan said. "But I figured that I'd better make sure that nothing happened to Chou. It's not likely the Thai syndicate would be willing to make a better deal with me. I also figured you might be a pretty useful connection as well, so I didn't want you to get killed, either."

"That was a very wise decision, Baum. Unlike talking to Joan Wing earlier today, which wasn't so smart," Radke said.

"Joan Wing? Is that the young woman who spoke to me at the hotel? Real pretty. She acted like she might be a reporter," Bolan said innocently.

"She's a reporter, all right, and a real troublemaker," he replied. "What did she want with you?"

"What else would a reporter want? She's looking for some information for a story. I thought she'd followed me into the hotel for a completely different reason. I was really disappointed to find out she was only interested in asking questions."

"We have to do something about that woman, Carson," Finley broke in. "She just won't back off."

"I know. What exactly did she ask you about, Baum?"

Bolan didn't want to say anything that would put Joan Wing's life in danger, so his reply was guarded.

"She asked what I knew about the U.S. Embassy security meeting with the Triad gangsters," Bolan said. "I didn't get the impression she knew any more than that. Of course I didn't say anything to her except to warn her to keep out of my business."

"If she approaches you again, I want you to tell her you're going to be meeting with me and you'll contact her after you've spoken with me," Radke said. "Make her give you a phone number where you can get in touch with her."

"Fine. Now, is there anywhere we can get some supper? We never did get that duck," Bolan said, changing the subject.

"Hell, Baum, how can you think about eating after all the blood we saw tonight?" Finley asked, his face still beaded with sweat.

"Because *I'm* still alive. We survived, and I certainly don't feel guilty about that. That's a lesson I learned from the war."

"Well, you're certainly a survivor," Radke said. "And a very good shot. Maybe you can give me some lessons in combat shooting."

"Yeah, and you and Leung can teach me some martial arts."

"You seemed to handle yourself pretty well, but I'd be happy to show you some stuff. A man with your skills and expertise is very valuable. In fact, you may be working more for us than for Chou," Radke continued. "Don't worry about the money. It'll pay very well, and you'll actually be doing something more worthwhile than running guns or smuggling heroin. If I read you right, Baum, you're still a patriot, despite how you got screwed over in Nam and in the States when you got back.''

"A patriot, huh? What sort of patriotism do you expect from me?" Bolan asked.

"We'll discuss that later," Radke promised. "We're almost at your hotel. Just don't make any plans after noon, tomorrow, okay?"

16

The morning edition of the *Bangkok Gazette* finally led with a story that didn't deal with Vietnam or Laos, the threat of war or Arlon Shaver's return to the United States. The headline instead read that a local restaurant had burned to the ground, and so far twenty-three charred bodies had been found among the debris. Bolan wasn't surprised to learn this referred to the China Jewel.

Although the corpses were badly burned and some might never be identified, the police had been able to determine that a number of the dead had been shot. They had learned gunfire had been heard in the area, and the slaughter was attributed to an ongoing gang war between rival criminal outfits. No mention was made of the Triad and Chou, nor were there any eyewitness reports of vehicles or individuals at the site.

Although the police might be withholding information from the press, Bolan doubted many people would be willing to disclose very much, due to fear of the Triad. For his part, he wasn't worried about the police coming after him, unless someone like Joan Wing had decided to stake out the China Jewel again, and had actually seen Bolan emerge with Radke and Finley.

He hoped Wing had the good sense and survival instincts to get out of Thailand before Radke and the Triad had her killed. The woman was obviously intelligent, but her professional idealism and stubbornness might keep her from protecting herself, even though she had to have realized she was in danger.

Bolan couldn't do anything to help Joan Wing. He had a mission to take care of, and so far he'd played his role well. Both Radke and Chou now trusted him. The gun battle had worked in Bolan's favor. There was nothing like a life-or-death situation to bring people together.

Bolan scanned the rest of the newspaper. An investigative team, assembled by the United Nations, was due to arrive in Thailand shortly. The editorial complained that this would be a waste of time, claiming that Vietnam and Laos were clearly the aggressors and there was no need for outsiders to interfere and to try to make some sort of compromise that could only benefit the Communists. What was needed was for the President of the United States to stop stalling and uttering vague, weak statements and take a firm stand against the threat of Communist expansion in Southeast Asia.

This was one time when Mack Bolan hoped the President would continue to do nothing, thereby giving him enough time to accomplish his mission. Bolan had made a lot of progress in a short time, but he'd made it by capitalizing on some good luck and without trying to push the enemy too much. He'd let Radke and Chou set the pace while he played along. The President might have to endure a lot of pressure and criticism, but Bolan could fail in his mission and lose his life if he became careless.

The Executioner left the hotel and stepped into the street. He had the morning to himself before the conspirators would come for him. He strolled along, for a brief moment enjoying the sights and sounds of Bangkok—from the rows of stores to the sidewalk merchants, where bolts of Thai silk, flatware and semiprecious jewelry were on display.

Bolan knew that he was probably being watched. The CIA agents and the Triad seemed to know every move he'd made and everyone he'd talked to since he'd arrived.

Although not given to souvenir shopping, Bolan did find a couple of things he could use. In a small curio shop, he found a hardwood walking stick with an ornate serpent design carved into it, the snake's body making up the shaft, its heart-shaped head serving as the handle. Bolan conducted the usual ritual of haggling over the price with the shopowner before they agreed on a sum.

The Executioner also bought a Bowie-style, single-edged knife, roughly the same size and weight as a Ka-bar combat knife. The handle was wood, with carved finger grooves, while the thick blade was made of good quality steel. A leather belt sheath came with the knife.

Back at the hotel, Bolan practiced his stick and knife fighting techniques while he waited for Radke's call.

Suddenly the phone rang. Bolan picked up the receiver, immediately recognizing Carson Radke's voice.

"I hope you enjoyed your little shopping trip today." Without waiting for a reply, Radke went on, "In half an hour walk by the shops you visited earlier."

He then hung up.

THIRTY MINUTES LATER, Bolan was strolling along the street once more. He kept an eye on the traffic but hadn't yet seen Radke's car. A crowd had formed on the corner, with people clustered around a Buddhist priest. The man chanted, and the crowd repeated his words. The congregation grew steadily larger, and people spilled over into the street, forcing traffic to slow down.

"Baum!" came a voice from a blue Buick.

Bolan turned to see Radke's face at the window. The car door opened, and he got into the back alongside Radke. Bob Noble sat in the driver's seat with Paul Finley beside him. No Triad, Bolan noticed. This was strictly a Company car.

"What the hell are those people doing?" Noble complained as he tried to steer around the crowd.

"Take it easy, Bob," Radke said. "It looks like they're having a prayer meeting."

"Ain't that swell," Noble muttered.

"Okay, Baum," Radke said, ignoring Noble, "you packing that Israeli cannon? And how about the big knife you bought today?"

"Of course," Bolan answered. "You think I'm going to be unarmed after what happened last night?"

"For now, I'd like you to give me those weapons, and the letter opener. You'll get them back later."

"I sure hope we don't get attacked by more of those Thai hoods," Bolan said. "I have a lot more faith in my ability with a gun than in yours, Radke."

Nevertheless, Bolan surrendered his Desert Eagle, the Bowie-style knife and the letter opener. Radke placed the weapons on the floor of the car by his feet.

They continued to head along the coast. Soon they had left Bangkok behind, and trees and tall grass began to replace the buildings and crowds of the city. After a few miles Noble turned off the main road and onto a dirt trail that hugged the bay.

"Where the hell are we going?" Bolan asked.

"Relax, Baum," Radke said. "I wouldn't bring you all the way out here just to kill you."

The Executioner didn't have to wait long to learn their destination. Soon, the car came to a small harbor. There were only two buildings: a simple two-story structure that stood by the plankwalk and a large tar-roof shack. A single boat occupied the little cove. An old pickup truck was parked outside the main building.

The Buick rolled onto the plankwalk and came to a halt. Two Asian males emerged from the main building, wearing T-shirts, shorts and sandals.

Radke stepped out of the car. The Asians greeted him with bows and a verbal welcome. Bolan guessed their language to be either Mandarin or Cantonese, not Thai. Radke spoke with them in their own tongue before he gestured for the others to get out of the car.

"These fellows are the caretakers," the Company man explained. "I picked them myself. They were peasants in southern China who used to work as part-time mules for the Triad. They don't understand English or Thai or any language except their own, and they can't read anything, even Cantonese. They're basically very simple and rather ignorant."

"And you want them to stay that way," Bolan remarked dryly.

"Absolutely," Radke replied. "They've been in this place since they arrived in Thailand. They're living better here—enough food, plenty of rice wine and about once a month we take them to a neighboring village for some recreation, if you get my drift."

"What about the truck?"

"Neither of them can drive. The truck doesn't run anyway. It's here for show, mainly. Someone might get curious about two foreigners living at a place like this, with no transportation. However, no one has stopped here except us, according to these two. They're too unsophisticated to be good liars."

"You must have something here you want guarded that you don't even want the guards to know about."

"Exactly, Baum," the CIA officer confirmed. "And we're about to share part of it with you."

"I'm honored," Bolan replied. "What is it?"

"You'll see. First, let's get rid of these two. Bob, take them out for a couple hours," Radke said to Noble.

The man nodded and returned to the car. Radke spoke to the Chinese before they, too, got into the vehicle. Once the Buick had pulled away from the pier, Radke led Bolan and Finley to the two-story building. The front room held some simple furniture, a small stove and a refrigerator.

They moved along a corridor until they came to a row of steel doors, each with a combination lock affixed above its handle. Radke stood in front of one and began to punch in a coded number.

"High security doors," he explained. "They won't open unless you know the right combination. If anybody forces a door, it will set off an explosion that'll blow this whole building to hell."

He opened the door, and they entered a small room with cardboard boxes stacked on shelves and a dozen ceramic turtles set out on two more shelves. Radke took down one of the turtles and held it out to Bolan. It looked fairly lifelike, with the head and feet painted dark gray and the shell mud brown.

"Cute," Bolan said. "You going into the curio business on the side?"

Radke smiled and reached into the turtle's hollow shell. Its legs began to move like a real turtle's. Radke turned the figure over onto its back to point out a simple framework of rods extending to the limbs, powered by a small clockwork system in the center.

"Before Bob joined the CIA he used to work for his father's toy company," Radke said. "It wasn't hard for him to make these for us."

"And what do you plan to do with them?"

"You're a smart guy, Baum. Take a guess."

"Let's see. Each turtle is large enough to carry probably a quarter of a kilo of a powerful plastic explosive such as C-4. With its dull color, it would be almost invisible at night. Plus it wouldn't be likely to alarm anyone who did see a turtle crawling along the ground. I guess it could be used to carry a transmitter, but I'd say it's better suited for a covert bomb delivery."

"Congratulations! I thought you'd get it," Radke said. "Paul makes the explosives, Bob the turtles and I pick the targets."

"Interesting," Bolan remarked. "Have you tried these things to see if they work?"

"You bet they were tested," Finley boasted. "And they worked perfectly. You might have heard about it. One exploded in Thailand and another in Laos awhile back."

Bolan pretended to be confused, and it was a few seconds before he spoke.

"The border firefight that occurred a day or two before Shaver was discovered," he said slowly. "You guys started it. So when the two little turtles went off, both sides thought they were under attack and all hell broke loose."

"Bingo," Finley said. "You got it."

"So then Vietnam would move in to support Laos's struggle against Thailand, and that could lead to a new U.S. military involvement in Southeast Asia. That's exactly what you want, isn't it?" Bolan went on.

"You put it all together very well, Baum," Radke replied. "Look, I don't have to tell you about those damned Communists. You fought them and tried to keep them from gaining ground by driving them back to the North. But American politics kept you from doing your job. You went home to an ungrateful country while the Reds claimed Laos and Cambodia as well as all of Vietnam. They'd move into Thailand tomorrow if they figured they could get away with it. We're going to force their hand, and this time the Commies will be on the losing end."

"So you want another war in Vietnam, and this time you think Washington will let our side win," Bolan said. "Maybe you know more than I do, because I'm not so sure that'll work."

"That doesn't really matter," Radke replied. "What it will do is increase support for the U.S. military and necessary Intelligence operations in Southeast Asia. We need a strong CIA network here. Our national security depends on that."

Radke's tone became more strident. "We must be on our guard against them. It's better to force Washington to set up the Intelligence and military forces necessary to contain this threat now, rather than to wait for our country to become weaker while the enemy gets stronger."

Bolan said nothing for a moment. Radke was obviously convinced his actions were patriotic and noble. The soldier knew he had to be careful about what he said.

"I can agree with all that," he began. "But how does the Triad come into this plan? I know Shaver was involved with heroin trafficking. Was he working for Chou when you found out about him?"

"Yeah. Shaver wanted to go back to the States as a hero, and we made it possible."

"And you think Shaver can convince everybody he really was a POW held captive by the

Vietnamese and Laotians all this time?'' Bolan asked.

"Shaver has been groomed for this event for months," Finley replied. "We literally held him prisoner. He was closed off from the light and almost starved to get into the right physical state. I personally injected diseases into his body. Damn near killed him, but he'll fool any medical examination. We pumped the stories of his 'hell in the tiger cages' so hard into his pea brain he probably believes it himself by now. We even tested him with a polygraph, and he fooled the lie detector. Believe me, Shaver is ready."

"You guys don't seem to miss much," Bolan said. "What about that attack on the military post by Laotian or Vietnamese troops? Did you stage that, too?"

"We got Chou to help us," Radke answered. "Leung and a few other Red Poles pretended to be Commie raiders. It worked pretty well, but none of them have the military expertise we'll need for future operations. That's why I'm glad you came along, Baum. You'll be perfect for our plans here."

"But what about the risks?" Bolan asked.

"I'll be in charge of CIA operations," Radke said. "My promotion to Director of Activities in Southeast Asia is beyond doubt. I'll tell everybody here what to do, and I'll tell Washington exactly what I want them to believe. And we'll all get rich and powerful while we save the United States of America at the same time."

"We'll get rich too?" Bolan inquired. "That sounds even better. How will that work?"

"We'll control everything that comes in and out of Thailand," Radke answered, "including the heroin and black market trades. This will allow Chou's syndicate to become the most powerful Triad in Southeast Asia, and we'll all get a piece of the action. We're talking about a slice of a pie that will net about two billion dollars a year in profit. Maybe more. So even a little slice is a hell of a lot of money, Baum."

"Sure is a lot more than I figured when I came to Thailand," Bolan said. "You bet I'm in. It's too good a deal to turn down."

"You're almost in," Radke corrected him. "But first I want you to do something to demonstrate your willingness to carry out any order, regardless of how distasteful you might find it to be. So you have to pass a little test for me."

"What kind of test?" Bolan asked with a frown.

"When Bob gets back we'll return to Bangkok. Then I'd like you and Bob to pay a visit on Miss Joan Wing. You remember her, don't you?"

Bolan nodded.

"Well, I want you to be the one to kill her when Bob's done with her," Radke said, his voice emotionless. "I tried to get her to back off, but she wouldn't. Joan Wing is a threat to us, and she has to be terminated."

17

"We're going to have some fun tonight," Bob Noble said with a grin.

Mack Bolan sat next to Noble in the front seat of the Buick. He wanted nothing more than to wipe that sadistic smile off the man's face, but instead, he remained silent, peering out the window. They had reached a poor neighborhood at the outskirts of Bangkok. Twilight had fallen, and the lack of streetlights left the area cloaked in darkness.

"No big talk, Baum?" Noble asked.

"Maybe I'll get more into the spirit of things when we get there," Bolan replied laconically.

The CIA agent killed the car's headlights as they rolled to a stop in an alley. They entered a shabby, dark building, and Noble led Bolan through a narrow corridor to a door at the end of the hall. After Noble had knocked on the door and uttered something in Thai, it was opened by a young man dressed in gray work clothes. His long black hair hung around his lean face, and an arrogant sneer twisted his thin lips. He locked the door behind the two men.

Another tough-looking young Thai rose from a chair. A ratty black beard covered his lower face, and he wore a similar gray outfit. The room wasn't very large and contained little furniture. Joan Wing sat tied to one of the three available chairs, the ropes crisscrossing her chest and lap. A cloth gag had been stuffed into her mouth. One of her eyes was bruised and swollen shut; the other watched the men with undisguised fear.

"She been any trouble, Lek?" Noble asked as he removed his jacket.

"She put up a fight when we grabbed her on the street, but there wasn't much she could do after we got her tied up. We were told to wait for you before we really started to work on her."

"Good," Noble said. He stepped up to Wing and tilted her chin. He stared at her.

"You had your chance to get away and you didn't take it, honey. Nobody really wanted to hurt you. Such a pretty little thing, too." He sounded almost apologetic.

Suddenly he rammed his clenched fist under her jaw in a short uppercut. Wing's head recoiled from the blow. Tears trickled down her cheeks, the gag keeping her silent. Noble laughed shortly.

"Before you knock her out, maybe we should ask her a couple of questions," Bolan said as he stepped forward.

"The hell with that," Noble replied. "She'd probably lie anyway."

Bolan moved between Noble and Wing. "There's something I want you to consider, Bob."

"What?"

The soldier kicked him in the groin. Anger fueled his attack, and the ball of his foot landed hard between Noble's legs. The agent gasped in pain, his eyes wide with surprise. Bolan moved in, smashing his bent elbow under Noble's jaw. The man's teeth clashed together, snipping off the tip of his tongue. He dropped to the floor, where he lay writhing in agony.

The Thais protested loudly, words Bolan didn't understand. He didn't need to. The bearded guy reached to the small of his back and drew a long-bladed dagger. The Executioner dodged the knife and lashed out a karate kick. The edge of his foot struck the man's wrist, sending the knife spinning from his grasp.

Bolan became aware of Lek rushing toward him. He quickly slammed a left hook to his adversary's bearded face, and as the guy's head bounced back, the Executioner grabbed his arm and propelled him into Lek. The hoods collided so hard that the impact forced them back several steps.

Noble began to make a move, but before he could draw the SIG-Sauer pistol from its shoulder leather, Bolan punched him in the face. Blood splashed from his cut lips, and two teeth rolled from his mouth. He collapsed to the floor, unconscious. Bolan knelt and yanked the gun from its holster.

By this time, Lek had shoved his stunned partner aside. He rushed for Bolan, a knife held ready in his fist. The soldier took aim and squeezed the trigger.

The SIG-Sauer roared in the confined area. Bolan saw the flash burst from the muzzle as the 9 mm bullet hit Lek in the chest. The upward path of the Parabellum round tunneled into his heart and sent the man reeling backward. Detecting a sudden movement out the corner of his eye, Bolan swung the pistol around. He saw the bearded Thai had grabbed a chair and was preparing to throw it at him.

The Executioner powered himself sideways and heard the chair smash into the wall behind him. He came up gripping the SIG-Sauer with both hands and aimed it at the Thai. He fired two rounds, then watched the man topple to the floor.

Bolan held his weapon at the ready, but neither thug stirred. Joan Wing sat in the chair, her unbruised eye fixed on Bolan.

"Don't worry," he said. "I'm one of the good guys. You're going to be okay."

Noble moaned, and Bolan turned in time to see him trying to unleather his pistol.

The soldier snapped off two shots from the SIG-Sauer. Noble's body jerked from the impact, then lay still.

"I'm sorry you had to see that, Ms. Wing, but it had to be done," Bolan said. "Now, I'm going to remove your gag. Don't scream, okay?"

The woman looked up at him and nodded. Once he'd removed the gag, she swallowed hard and asked an expected question.

"Who are you?"

Bolan cut her ropes as he spoke. "I go by the name of Patrick Baum," he said. "I know about Radke, the Triad and the conspiracy. Can you stand?"

Wing rose from the chair. Her legs were somewhat unsteady, but she seemed to have survived the experience as well as could be expected.

"You were right about Radke and this whole situation," Bolan stated. "But it's even bigger than you suspected. I'll have to fill you in later."

He turned to Noble's corpse and quickly frisked him, coming up with the keys to the car.

"What are we going to do?" Wing asked.

"First, we've got to get out of here. You don't write for a Thai paper, do you?"

"No, a Hong Kong publication."

"So, it'll be best to take you to the British embassy. You'll be safe there. Tell them everything that happened and everything you know."

"But what about you?" Wing asked.

"When Radke realizes he's in trouble, he'll need to take care of some damning evidence, and I know where he'll go. I'm going to try to get there in time to stop him."

"You can't go alone."

"There isn't time to get backup," Bolan replied.

He headed for the door, Wing following. He edged out into the corridor, the pistol held ready. The hall was empty. Somewhere in the building Bolan heard a baby cry and a number of voices from the nearby rooms. The gunshots had obviously not gone unheard, but no one cared to venture outside to investigate. Bolan escorted Wing from the building and to the alley where the Buick was parked.

"Let me drive," she said. "I probably know the city better than you do."

"If you're up to it." Bolan handed her the keys, and she slid behind the steering wheel. He got in beside her. Wing started the engine and backed out of the alley. In moments they rolled onto the street.

Bolan noticed she drove well and seemed to have handled her unpleasant experience okay. A tough lady.

As if reading his thoughts, Wing spoke. "Thank you for saving my life. I was pretty terrified back there."

"Don't think about it. It's over now and you just have to concentrate on getting to the embassy."

"Fair enough," she replied with a little laugh. "I'll concentrate on driving, and you stay ready to kill any bad guys."

THEIR JOURNEY through the streets of Bangkok seemed to take forever, but Wing actually covered the distance to the British embassy fairly quickly. Traffic wasn't heavy, and Bolan didn't see any vehicles following them. So far their luck seemed to be holding up.

Wing stopped the car at the gates to the embassy.

"Come in with me," she urged. "I'm sure somebody here will help you."

"It'll take too long for them to take action," Bolan replied. "Bureaucrats are the same everywhere. They'll talk and talk and move along a chain of command and try to cover their backs. I'd welcome a unit of SAS commandos, but I'm afraid I'll have to handle this on my own."

Wing suddenly leaned toward him and pressed her lips briefly to Bolan's mouth. Then she pulled back and appeared to be about to say something. But clearly no words seemed appropriate. She got out of the car and headed for the embassy gates.

Bolan slid behind the wheel, waiting until he'd seen her safely escorted through the gates before driving off.

He'd barely covered a single city block when a beer truck suddenly pulled out from an alley to block his path. Bolan swerved to avoid the vehicle, but a second beer truck had filled the lane next to him so that he was forced to turn the wheel again. The Buick skidded, its tail connecting with the side of the first truck as Bolan struggled to keep the car from crashing.

The car's front tires hopped the curb, and the nose of the Buick smashed into a newsstand. Plywood burst on impact, and papers and magazines fell across the windshield. Bolan hit the brakes, and the car slammed lengthwise into a solid object. He peered out the side window and saw several figures rushing toward the crippled car. One of them held a bottle in his fist, a burning rag stuck in the glass neck revealing his intentions.

Bolan opened the car door and dived from the vehicle. He hit the sidewalk in a shoulder roll and scrambled away from the Buick. The sound of glass shattering and a roar of heat announced that the Molotov cocktail had hit the car.

Bolan sprinted for cover at the rear of the truck, firing off three quick rounds. He saw a figure fall, but the others responded with gunfire, so that bullets sang ricochet tunes against a brick wall near him. Flames crackled around the car, and in the flickering glare Bolan spotted two armed opponents blocking his path at the rear of the truck.

Bolan snap aimed, then squeezed off a shot, the 9 mm slug punching through the forehead of a gunner. The other man raised a Beretta M-12 submachine gun as the soldier dropped to one knee and triggered the pistol twice. The subgunner loosed a burst, and bullets sparked along the sidewalk less than two feet from Bolan. A ricochet slug tugged at the Executioner's jacket, then the hardman dropped his weapon and doubled up, two Parabellum rounds in his belly.

A shape moved by the edge of the truck. Bolan triggered his pistol, but a click told him he was out of ammo. He tossed the empty SIG-Sauer and made a grab for the Beretta subgun lying on the ground. His fingers were on the steel frame when the shock wave from the explosion struck him like a giant paddle. He just had time to realize that the gas tank had blown before a black fog fell across his senses.

18

The first thing Mack Bolan was aware of when he came to was that he couldn't feel his arms. He shifted one foot, then the other. His ankles weren't restricted. A dull pain throbbed at the back of his head.

Bolan inhaled slowly, his eyes still closed. He tried to determine what condition he was in and couldn't detect any broken bones or serious injury. He realized his hands were cuffed behind his back. The sound of an engine and a rolling motion suggested he was inside a vehicle. Bolan slowly opened his eyes, relieved to discover his vision was clear. The angry face of an Asian stared directly back at him.

The man's arm rose, but before he could deliver a blow, Bolan heard someone speak. The man dropped his arm. The soldier glanced about and saw he was flanked by beer kegs.

Wooden floorboards lay beneath him. He was in the back of a beer truck.

"Mr. Baum?" a voice inquired politely.

Leung's face appeared in Bolan's line of vision.

"Chan is upset because you killed a friend of his," the Red Pole explained. "I told him to leave you alone."

"Thanks," Bolan said. "I appreciate that, Mr. Leung."

"Do not expect too much kindness. Mr. Radke wants you alive for interrogation. I doubt that will be pleasant. I understand you killed Bob Noble."

"Yeah."

"Good," Leung said. "He deserved to die. I do not generally enjoy killing a person, but I would have been glad to kill that one myself. If I have to kill you, I will try to make it as quick and painless as possible."

Bolan smiled wryly. "Under the circumstances, what more could I expect?"

The next few minutes passed in silence. The truck came to a halt. Leung and Chan drew Bolan to his feet and helped him from the rig. He came face-to-face with Carson Radke, Paul Finley directly behind him.

"Hello, Baum. I guess you had a busy night," Radke said, sneering. "Actually I've got to give you credit. You really had me fooled with this act of yours."

He suddenly drove a fist into Bolan's solar plexus, the blow knocking the wind from his lungs.

"Carson," Finley said, "let me handle this."

"All right," the CIA officer agreed. "You make him talk first, then I'll kill him."

As Leung and Chan escorted Bolan away from the truck, he realized that they had brought him to the hidden pier that had been his intended destination. He just hadn't expected to arrive as a prisoner.

"You're not so smart really, Baum," Radke declared as they marched toward the main building. "If you'd been clever, you would've killed that woman like I told you to. Then I would've really trusted you and let you in on everything."

"You've told me enough to know you're willing to get thousands of people killed just so you can get in a commanding position," Bolan said. "You can claim your motives are patriotic or anti-Communist, but it's really just personal ambition and greed, Radke."

"Spare me the sermon. All I need to know is who sent you and how much they know."

"He'll talk, Carson," Finley promised. "You know you can't rely on his telling the truth. My way is better. You might as well save your breath for now."

They entered the main building. Bolan saw the two Chinese caretakers lying on the floor near the stove. Fresh bloodstains by their heads told him they'd been killed quite recently. Radke waved a hand at the corpses.

"I had to get rid of them as potential witnesses. It was a shame, because I really liked them. I liked you, too, Baum." There was a note of his regret in his voice.

They moved along the corridor to the row of steel security doors. Finley headed for the last door and punched in a combination to unlock it.

"You know about our explosive turtles," Radke said, "but we didn't show you what's behind the other doors. Here is our computer room."

"I figured you're dealing with so many crooked deals, unauthorized Intelligence and covert bank accounts that you had to keep records somehow. A computer works better than filing cabinets.''

"Well, you guessed right again, Baum. Of course, this system isn't connected to any mainframe that might allow us to be tapped and scanned by any other computer systems out there.''

"So you have all sorts of special information on floppy disks?'' Bolan asked. "You plan to take them with you?''

"Who said we were leaving?''

"You wouldn't have murdered the caretakers if you hadn't decided this site has been compromised. You're probably leaving Thailand as well, right?''

"Actually that's thanks to you, Baum,'' Radke said. "Maybe you'll find some satisfaction in the knowledge you altered our plans, but at least Paul and I will be living as rich expatriates with new identities, new faces and millions of dollars to help us deal with our disappointment. Meantime, you'll be dead.''

"Carson,'' Finley broke in, "let's get this interrogation over with. We don't have all night.''

"Right. Leung, you go with Paul and make sure Baum doesn't try anything. I've got some packing to do. Chan and Hsin will make sure the boat is ready. We're going for a midnight cruise. We should be in Singapore or Indonesia sometime tomorrow afternoon."

"Come on, Baum," Finley said. "It's time for a little chat."

BOLAN DISCOVERED what was behind the last security door. It led to a basement that contained three cells surrounding a small bay section, with a single wooden chair bolted to the stone floor. Wrist and ankle straps were attached to the chair. Finley took a leather pouch from his jacket pocket and unzipped it. Inside was a syringe and two small vials of liquid.

"You ever hear of scopolamine?" he asked. "This is the most reliable truth serum known to man. It can also be dangerous. Too large a dose can kill you. So let's hope the first dose does the job, because if I have to give you another you might not survive it."

"Radke is going to kill me anyway," Bolan said.

"Nobody lives forever, Baum. But it's how you die that makes a difference. So don't make this any harder than it has to be."

Finley drew his SIG-Sauer and pointed it at Bolan while Leung stepped behind him to unlock the handcuffs. The Executioner offered no resistance as Leung removed the manacles. He sat in the chair, placing his hands on the armrests by the straps.

Leung moved to his right side while Finley holstered his pistol and stepped to the left. As they prepared to buckle the straps around his wrists, Leung looked at Bolan and shook his head.

"I really am sorry," he said.

"Yeah," Bolan replied. "Me, too."

The Executioner suddenly swung with his left arm, breaking free of Finley's hold before the CIA agent could get a firm grip. Bolan's fist then hit Leung in the middle of his face, sending him reeling back. Finley cursed and reached for his pistol.

Bolan gripped the armrest with his right hand for balance as he lashed out high with his left leg, slamming his heel into Finley's jaw. The kick hurled the Company man against the stone wall, and he fell facefirst, unconscious, to the floor. The soldier started to turn toward Leung and caught a rock-solid backfist stroke to the side of his face, the blow spinning him.

The Red Pole slashed his arm in a high arch, his hand poised to connect with Bolan's neck. The Executioner raised his arm to block the deadly stroke. Leung's other hand snapped forward, the fingers pressed into a crane-beak formation aimed for Bolan's eye. The soldier slapped the hand aside with his right palm, turning with the movement and lashing a roundhouse kick under Leung's ribs.

The man went down. Bolan doubted his tough adversary was really hurt, so was prepared when Leung whirled his extended leg in a low sweep, aiming for Bolan's ankles. He jumped clear of the "iron broom" technique, but Leung swiftly rose from the floor and pumped both fists into the Executioner's chest.

The double punch propelled Bolan backward into a wall. Leung advanced quickly and thrust a powerful side kick for Bolan's abdomen. The warrior dodged the attack, and Leung's foot struck the wall hard. The room seemed to reverberate from the impact of the blow. Too skilled to be thrown off track by a miss, Leung lashed out at Bolan's face.

The Executioner ducked the attack and snared Leung's wrist with one hand. His other hand grabbed the fingers of Leung's open palm. He bent them back while he pressed on Leung's wrist. Bone crunched, and the Red Pole screamed as all four fingers snapped. Bolan then swung a kick at the small of his adversary's back, driving him facefirst into the wall.

Leung started to sag, but Bolan knew he couldn't afford to take chances with such a dangerous opponent. He wrapped his arm around the man's neck, his forearm jammed against Leung's windpipe. Bolan braced his other arm across the base of the enforcer's skull, securing a viselike grip. One hard twist, a crack of bone and Leung slumped to the floor, his head dangling on the stem of his broken neck.

Bolan breathed hard as he stepped away from the man's corpse. His body felt as if he'd been stomped on by an angry mule, and the side of his face ached. He walked over to Finley and rolled him onto his back. He found the guy's SIG-Sauer and yanked it from the shoulder holster.

Finley moaned as he started to regain consciousness. Bolan slapped the steel barrel of the pistol across the man's already battered jaw. Finley fell limp and silent once more.

A sound drew Bolan's attention to the stairs. He looked up and saw Carson Radke standing in the doorway, his arm extended and a pistol in his hand.

19

Mack Bolan threw himself to one side an instant before two shots rang out from the stairwell. He came up into a kneeling stance and returned fire with Finley's SIG-Sauer. He couldn't see Radke, but he hoped that a couple of 9 mm slugs would deter him from remaining at the head of the stairs.

There was no return fire from Radke.

As Bolan slowly moved to the foot of the stairs, his pistol held ready, he noticed a scarlet stain spreading across Finley's shirtfront. One of Radke's bullets had struck his fellow CIA agent.

Bolan edged up the stairs, his eyes fixed on the doorway. He pressed his back against the door and peered through the narrow space between the frame and the hinges to be certain Radke wasn't lying in wait behind the open door.

A bullet struck the steel door and whined against the metal. Bolan ducked and fired back in the direction of the shot, at the same time spying Radke's retreating figure moving down the corridor, a pistol clutched in one hand, a metal suitcase in the other. In response the Company officer triggered two hasty shots back at Bolan. They went wild, but Radke made it around the corner into the front room.

Bolan advanced stealthily. He had a clear view of the front door and could see if Radke tried to escape by that route. However, there was a large window in the front room that Radke could climb out of. He noticed one of the security doors standing open. He trained his pistol on the threshold as he edged along the hallway.

A figure suddenly appeared in the doorway, revolver in hand. Bolan immediately pumped two Parabellum rounds into the gunman's chest. He slid down against the doorframe, his eyes still open and his mouth forming in a small oval of surprise.

Bolan paused long enough to scoop up the dead man's handgun. It was an old .38 Special Colt revolver, and the Executioner stuck it in his belt as backup. He recognized the dead man. He was the other Chinese Red Pole, Hsin, Chan's partner.

Two shots rang out from the end of the corridor as Radke stuck his arm around the corner and fired. A bullet tore into a wall near Bolan, while the other round whistled into the hallway. The warrior returned fire and saw a chunk of plaster go flying from the corner's edge when his 9 mm bullet struck the spot where Radke's hand had been an instant before.

"You really are a lousy shot, Radke," Bolan called out. "Do you know you killed your buddy Paul when you missed me in the basement?" He used the sound of his voice to cover his move to the next room. He glanced about him and saw the turtles lined along the shelves. He also noticed a small battery-operated clock on another shelf that was connected to two boxes by a number of wires. A closer investigation revealed the components: the timer, attached to a detonator, and plastic explosives. Clearly they were the late Paul Finley's homemade explosives.

So Radke intended to blow up the building after he'd fled the area. In fact there were enough explosives to destroy the entire pier. However, it was a simple setup, and Bolan merely had to disconnect the detonator wires from the box charging device to deactivate the bomb.

He crept out into the corridor, slowly advancing toward the front room. A sudden creak on the wooden stairs that led to the second floor of the building warned him that someone was there, just out of view.

He ducked and swung around the corner, the SIG-Sauer aimed up the staircase. He squeezed the trigger before he even saw the man on the steps. His shot was true. Mortally wounded, the man dropped his weapon and tumbled down the steps, landing on the floor near Bolan's feet. It was another unfamiliar face, and Bolan wondered how many more Chou Red Poles were lurking in the area.

There was no response from Radke to this latest shooting, but Bolan's entrance into the front room was cautious. He stayed low, the pistol gripped in both hands as he scanned the area. The open window revealed that Radke had fled the building.

He'd just begun to get to his feet when a figure charged through the front door, flames spewing from the muzzle of his weapon as full-auto fire sprayed the walls of the room.

Bolan swiftly assumed a low kneeling stance as slugs slashed the air above his head. He aimed the SIG-Sauer and squeezed the trigger twice. Both Parabellum rounds plowed into his opponent's belly, and the guy doubled up with a loud groan. Bolan trained his pistol on the man's bowed head and fired another round. The 9 mm projectile split the top of the guy's skull like a ripe melon. He slid to the floor, and his automatic rifle slipped from his lifeless fingers.

The Executioner smiled when he recognized the weapon—an M-16 assault rifle. He picked up the weapon. The triggerman had probably burned up half the ammo, but there were still about fifteen 5.56 mm shells left in the box-shaped magazine.

This time he knew the face—Chan would no longer be a problem. But Carson Radke still was.

Bolan stepped out of the building. Radke was kneeling at the pier, in the process of untying the boat from its post. The soldier raised the M-16 to his shoulder and triggered a controlled 3-round burst. The slugs splintered the wood along the post.

Radke jumped back, startled by the unexpected attack. Bolan fired the autorifle and scored three more bullets into the plankwalk near the CIA agent's feet.

"Give up or get killed," Bolan announced. "Either way is okay with me."

The Company man bolted for the supply shack. Bolan fired three rounds at the wooden structure as a deterrent. Radke ignored the threat and hurled himself at the door. It burst open and he tumbled inside, disappearing from Bolan's view.

The Executioner edged over to the beer truck parked in the center of the plankwalk and used it for cover. All was silent except for the ripple of water in the cove.

"Hey, Radke," he called, "you're boxed in. I can wait for you to make a move, but it'll be easier for me to take you out than the other way around. This rifle gives me more range than a pistol, and I'm a better marksman than you."

Radke cursed loudly, and Bolan realized that he was losing his edge. That was good if it forced the man to surrender, but not so good if it made him desperate enough to try anything.

"I figure we'll have company soon," Bolan said. "Joan Wing reached the British embassy. You're finished, Radke. All that's left is to find out whether you'll still be breathing after this is over."

Radke didn't respond for almost a minute. Bolan had begun to wonder if perhaps the man had escaped from a window at the rear of the shack or if there was a trapdoor that led under the pier, when Radke called out.

"Hey, Baum! I'm throwing out my gun. Okay?"

The pistol sailed out from the door of the shack and landed on the plankwalk.

"I'm coming out!" Radke announced. "Don't shoot!"

He stood in the doorway, both hands raised to shoulder level. Bolan trained the M-16 on him and slowly approached.

"That's a good start," he began. "Now, keep your hands up, step forward, then get down on your knees on the plankwalk."

The strong smell of gasoline wafted out from the shack. "Don't you smell anything, Baum?" Radke asked. "See, I spilled fuel from the supply tank inside. A single spark, like one caused by a bullet, will set it off. This place will go up in flames and ignite the oxygen tanks for scuba diving stored here. That means we'll have a nice big explosion."

"Then I guess I'd better back off again," Bolan said.

"Do you know what I had in that case I was carrying?" Radke continued. "The floppy disks from our computer. It has records about Shaver and Chou, contacts I had with other CIA operatives, mercenaries, bank accounts and all that stuff. You'll have proof I was behind the conspiracy and that Shaver is a fraud. You'll be able to prevent military aggression by the U.S., Vietnam and Laos. It'll make you a real big hero.

"But you're going to have to come and get it, Baum. As I said, though, if you try to shoot me, there's a good chance you'll set off the gasoline."

"I wonder whether there really is any scuba gear in there," Bolan said.

"Then go ahead and shoot," Radke invited as he reached back down to pick up the case. He smiled at Bolan and patted the metal container.

"Come and get it," he urged. "Put down your guns and see if you can take me hand-to-hand. If you win, you get the big brass ring of the decade. If you lose, well..." His smile grew wider.

Bolan tossed aside the M-16. He drew the SIG-Sauer from his belt and finally the Colt .38 revolver, placing them on the plankwalk and entering the shack empty-handed. Radke nodded his approval, the case still in his hand.

"I've got to give you credit, Baum. You've got guts," Radke murmured.

The Company man suddenly hurled the case at Bolan, who raised his arm to block the hard metal projectile, and charged. His palm smacked into the side of Bolan's head, the blow causing the Executioner to stagger against a large metal drum. Gasoline splashed over his feet.

Radke pounced from behind. One hand grabbed Bolan's hair, the other snared the back of his collar as he pumped a knee into the soldier's kidney. Bolan knew what Radke was about to do. He had seen the CIA agent break a man's neck with just such a head twist.

The Executioner quickly reached back, grabbing Radke's left wrist with one hand, finding his right hand with the other. Digging his fingers in, Bolan pushed his arms high, forcing Radke's arms as well. He then crossed his forearms, dropped to one knee and bent his back forward. The momentum sent Radke hurtling over Bolan's shoulder to crash to the gasoline-soaked floor.

Radke rolled back, braced himself up on his shoulders and lashed out at Bolan with both feet. The kick knocked the Executioner off-balance and sent him across the room into a wooden rowboat mounted on a pair of saw-horses. Bolan saw Radke jump to his feet and rush to another mounted rowboat. A fishnet draped the hull of the vessel, and a pole with a large hook on one end leaned against it.

"I'm going to rip your guts out!" Radke snarled, grabbing the pole with both hands.

Bolan glanced at the boat next to him. There was no hooked pole handy, but he did see an oar. He grabbed the shaft and arced the paddle end to block Radke's swing. Wood clashed with wood. The agent hissed a curse as he jabbed with the pole, trying to sink the hook into Bolan's neck.

The soldier raised the oar and struck with the edge of the paddle section across Radke's fingers. The man yelped with pain, and Bolan quickly delivered a buttstroke. The force of his blow ripped the weapon from Radke's weakened grasp.

Before Radke could collect his wits, Bolan thrust the rounded end of the oar into his belly, just below the solar plexus, then slammed the paddle end across his face. A final blow to the back of Radke's skull propelled his body across the net-strewn boat.

The Executioner stepped back, breathing hard. He glanced about the shack. There was some fishing gear in a corner, a diving mask, flippers and a speargun on a wooden shelf. There were no oxygen tanks.

As Bolan reached down for the case, Radke launched himself suddenly with a roar, with the fishing net clutched in his hands. He flung it over Bolan's head and shoulders, to close around him like a shroud.

Radke attacked with uncontrolled fury, blood oozing from his split mouth. Bolan tried to ward off the blows despite being restricted by the net. Radke managed to land a kick to his stomach and a fist to his skull above the right temple that dropped him to one knee.

Bolan gripped the oar with both hands and shoved it against the agent's shins like a bar. Radke lost his balance and crashed to the floor.

The Executioner pulled off the net. "Don't bother to get up," he said. "I'll find my own way out."

Bolan tossed the oar aside and picked up the case. He stepped outside and breathed deeply to clear the smell of gasoline. He collected the weapons he'd left on the plankwalk, sticking the pistol into his belt and tucking the M-16 under his arm. He held the Colt revolver in his hand as he looked back at the shack.

Radke was standing, framed in the doorway of the shack, the raised speargun in his hand.

Bolan knew that the Colt revolver could go off on impact after he cocked the hammer—a hard enough jar making the hammer fall. He judged the distance to the shack and hurled the revolver at the doorway. Bolan dashed for the cover of the truck as he heard the report of the .38 handgun. Radke's claim that a single spark would ignite the gasoline proved accurate. Flames erupted within the shack, followed almost instantaneously by an explosion as the gasoline tank blew, scattering burning debris across the harbor.

Bolan stayed low until he was sure the shower of fiery wreckage had ended. He opened the case and discovered it was packed with hundreds of bills in Thai, British, American and Swiss currencies. There was probably close to a million dollars, but this didn't matter to the Executioner. He then noticed something jammed into a cloth pocket in the lid of the case. He reached inside and pulled out several floppy disks. He'd hit the jackpot.

REPORTERS FROM A DOZEN countries surrounded the platform as Joan Wing concluded her press conference.

"The evidence that proves my claims about Carson Radke is already in the hands of the President of the United States and the director of the Central Intelligence Agency," Wing said. "It is important to understand that Mr. Radke was acting on his own and that the CIA wasn't involved." Wing clicked the button on the remote control, and the TV screen went blank.

She smiled at Bolan. "So, how did I do?"

"I figure you're going to be a big name in journalism circles. Your career's going to skyrocket. And you'll probably write a bestseller."

She frowned. "But there won't be any fame or glory for you, Patrick, will there? No one will know what you've done."

"I don't want fame or glory," Bolan assured her. "And the people who matter know."

"Do you still have to leave Bangkok and go back to the States?"

"Not until tomorrow," the Executioner replied. "Not until tomorrow."

Gold Eagle Presents
a special three-book in-line continuity

THE RED DRAGON TRILOGY

Beginning in June 1996, Gold Eagle brings you another action-packed three-book in-line continuity, The Red Dragon Trilogy.

In THE EXECUTIONER #210—FIRE LASH, book 1 of The Red Dragon Trilogy, The Triads and the Red Chinese have struck a bargain sealed in hell—with a quick payoff in escalating terrorism, murder and heroin traffic. But long-range plans include a conspiracy of terrifying global consequence.

Don't miss the first book of this new trilogy, available in June at your favorite retail outlet.

Adventure and suspense in the midst
of the new reality

Created by

JAMES AXLER

DEATH LANDS®

Circle Thrice

In the midst of the lawlessness and oppression of the twenty-second
century, it appears that peace and hope may start to flourish in
pockets of civilization called villes. But when Ryan Cawdor and
his band of warrior survivalists are guests of a powerful Tennessee
baroness, they find that her ville is home to an ages-old darkness.

**Bolan's war against an old enemy is dogged
by strange alliances—and even the Vatican
is not exempt**

DON PENDLETON's
MACK BOLAN.

An old-line mafioso's death and the abduction of the
capo's young great-grandson launches a turf war that
reaches all the way to Romania's most powerful crime boss.
Mack Bolan steps in, and his baptism by hellfire won't stop
until he's exacted the highest price from those who wage
war against the innocent. Justice is coming, and it will
be relentless....

**An old enemy develops a deadly
new train of thought...**

THE

Destroyer

#103 Engines of Destruction

Created by
WARREN MURPHY
and RICHARD SAPIR

The railways have become the fastest—and surest—way
to get from here to eternity. Could the repeated sightings
of a ghostly samurai swordsman be linked to the
high-speed derailments that are strewing the rails with
headless victims? Suspecting the train terror is merely a
decoy, Remo Williams and Master Chiun become
involved, only to find they may literally lose their heads
over an old enemy.

**A flare-up of hatred and violence
threatens to engulf America**

BLACK OPS #2

ARMAGEDDON NOW

created by MICHAEL KASNER

The Black Ops team goes where the law can't—to avenge acts
of terror directed against Americans around the world. But now
the carnage is the bloody handiwork of Americans as Los Angeles
turns into a powder keg in a sweeping interracial war. Deployed
to infiltrate the gangs, the Black Ops commandos uncover a
trail of diabolical horror leading to a gruesome vision of
social engineering....

Don't miss out on the action in these titles featuring
THE EXECUTIONER®, ABLE TEAM® and PHOENIX FORCE®!